Sarah Ellen Blackwell

A Military Genius

Life of Anna Ella Carroll, of Maryland, the Great Unrecognized Member of Lincoln's

Cabinet

Sarah Ellen Blackwell

A Military Genius
Life of Anna Ella Carroll, of Maryland, the Great Unrecognized Member of Lincoln's Cabinet

ISBN/EAN: 9783337232542

Printed in Europe, USA, Canada, Australia, Japan

Cover: Foto ©Raphael Reischuk / pixelio.de

More available books at **www.hansebooks.com**

LIFE OF ANNA ELLA CARROLL,

OF MARYLAND,

("The great unrecognized member of Lincoln's Cabinet.")

COMPILED FROM FAMILY RECORDS AND CONGRESSIONAL
DOCUMENTS

BY

SARAH ELLEN BLACKWELL.

For Sale at the Office of the *Woman's Journal*, 3 Park Street, Boston, Mass.
Rooms of the Woman's Suffrage Society, 1406 G St., Washington, D. C.

PRICE : $1.10 (Forwarded free on receipt of price).

WASHINGTON, D. C. :
JUDD & DETWEILER, PRINTERS.
1891.

The long years come and go,
　　And the Past,
The sorrowful splendid Past,
With its glory and its woe,
Seems never to have been.

　　Seems never to have been!
O somber days and grand,
How ye crowd back once more,
Seeing our heroes graves are green
By the Potomac, and the Cumberland
And in the valley of the Shenandoah!

When we remember how they died,
In dark ravine and on the mountain side,
In leaguered fort and fire-encircled town,
And where the iron ships went down.
How their dear lives were spent
In the weary hospital tent,
In the cockpit's crowded hive,
　　——— it seems
　Ignoble to be alive!

　　　　　　THOMAS BAILEY ALDRICH.

CONTENTS.

(v)

CHAPTER V.

CHAPTER VI.

CHAPTER VII.

CHAPTER VIII.

CHAPTER IX.

PREFACE.

In commencing the attempt to portray a very remarkable career I had hoped for the coöperation of the person concerned so far, at least, as the supervision of any statements I might find it necessary to make. But it was decided by her friends that it would not be well for her at present to be troubled with new projects, or even informed of them. It was at first a serious disappointment to me and seemed to increase my difficulties, but as I was allowed access to sources of family information I have been enabled to present a sketch, slight and inadequate, but authentic, and greatly desired by many distant friends. With continued improvement in health I trust that the wishes of Miss Carroll's friends may be better met by an autobiography taking the place of the present meager and imperfect sketch.

It should be at once understood that this is *not* a plea for Miss Carroll.

Her work has but to be fairly presented to speak for itself.

Her claim was settled once and forever by the evidence given before the first Military Committee of 1871, met to consider the claim, and reporting, through Senator Howard, unanimously endorsing every fact. The Assistant Sec-

retary of War, Thomas A. Scott, the Chairman of the
Committee for the Conduct of the War, Benjamin F. Wade,
and Judge Evans, of Texas, testifying in a manner that
was conclusive. These men knew what they were talking
about and human testimony could no farther go. Congress,
through its committees, has again and again endorsed the
claim, and never denied it, being "adverse" only to award
as involving national recognition.

Our great generals have left us one by one without ever
antagonizing the claim, and General Grant advised Miss
Carroll to continue to push her claim for recognition.

But this work is to be considered rather in the light of
an historical research bearing on questions of the day.

Are our present laws and customs just toward women?
Are women ever preëminently fitted for high offices in the
State? Is it for our honor and advantage when so fitted to
avail ourselves of the whole united intellect and moral
power of men and women side by side in peril and in duty?
Such a life as this gives to all these questions the authorita-
tive answer of established facts.

NEW YORK, *April 21st, 1891.* (Summer address, Law-
rence, Long Island, N. Y.)

Miss Carroll's address is 931 New Hampshire Avenue,
Washington, D. C.

———

Arriving as a stranger in Washington, knowing nothing of libraries and document rooms, Secretaries offices, and War departments, I was at first greatly at a loss. For many years I had had in my possession two very important documents, the last memorial of 1878 and the report of the Military Committee thereon under General Bragg in 1881. With these two in my hand I proceeded to consult the Descriptive Catalogue of the Congressional Library. To my surprise, I found that these two very important documents had been omitted from the index. Calling attention to the fact, we looked them up in the body of the volume and Mr. Spofford immediately added them in pencil together with the other important documents, in Miss Carroll's favor, which had also been omitted. When I made my way to the Senate document room I found that this important Miss. Doc. 58 had been omitted there also, having been set down under another name. Looking it up in the volume of Miscellaneous Documents I again obtained the admission by Mr. Amzi Smith. In the list at the Secretaries office Miss. Doc. 58 was also omitted together with the last report by a Military Committee, under General Bragg, endorsing the claim in the most thorough going way. The index ending with an intermediate report mistakenly designated as *adverse*, though the previous reports were not thus heralded as favorable.

After the first report, as made by Senator Howard and the repeated endorsements made by Wilson and Williams of succeeding Congresses, these two documents are by far the most important and interesting.

The memorial of '78, containing additional evidence explaining some things, otherwise unaccountable, and making some very singular revelations. It is a mine of wealth for the future historian. At the Secretary's office I showed the documents and stated that their exclusion must have been unfavorable to the presentation of the case. I was not equally fortunate in obtaining their immediate admission, but trust the mistake has since been rectified.

The report marked as "adverse" would be more truly described as "admission of the incontestable nature of the evidence in support of the claim," admitting the services in every particular and being "adverse" only to award involving national recognition.

At the Secretary's office I obtained permission to see the file of the 41st Congress, 2d. session. There I saw the first short memorial with the plan of campaign attached as described by Thomas Scott. Then my investigations were temporarily ended by the outside of a document being shown me stating that the papers had been withdrawn by Samuel Hunt, thus agreeing with the statement made by him in Miss. Doc. 58, that they had been stolen from his desk while the committee were examining the claim.

I found it very difficult to obtain the earlier documents.

" Supply exhausted " being the answer that has long been given, but all can be looked up in the bound volumes.

When, at length, fairly started in my work I was disturbed by a rumor that Miss Carroll's papers, formerly placed on file at the War Department, were no longer to be found there. I set out as far as possible to investigate. Provided with an excellent letter of introduction to the Secretary of War I made my way, on March 6, 1891, to the vast building of the War Department and sent in my letter with a list of the documents I wanted to see. Miss Carroll's Military papers, given in the Miss. Doc. 58, and a list of letters from the same memorial by Wade, Scott, and Evans.

The permission being kindly accorded I was transferred to the Record office and told that the file should be ready for me on the following day.

Taking with me the Miss. Doc. 58, an unpublished manuscript of Miss Carroll's, and specimens of the handwriting of Wade and Scott, I punctually put in an appearance, was transferred to the office of the Adjutant General, and Miss Carroll's file produced for my inspection. I met with all possible courtesy and every facility for the examination. I found two of the papers on my list in her now familiar handwriting, and some others.

A letter to Secretary Stanton, of May 14, 1862, recommending the occupation of Vicksburgh and referring to Pilot Scott, stating that she had derived from him some of the important information which had lead to her paper to the War Department on Nov. 30, 1861, which had occasioned the change of campaign in the southwest and proved of such incalculable benefit to the national cause.

A paper of May 15th, 1862, advising that Memphis and
Vicksburgh should be strongly occupied and the Yazoo river
watched. Another letter to Stanton concerning her pamphlets and proposing to write another one in aid of Mr. Lincoln, unjustly assailed. There was a portion of a letter
written in great haste from St. Louis. There was an interesting letter from Robert Lincoln when Secretary of War.
A petition from a group of ladies, asking for information
concerning Miss Carroll's services and several other documents, but most of the important papers on my list were
not on the file.

After examining the papers for some time I asked to see
the originals of the letters of Wade and Scott. I was told
they were in another department and would take some
time to look up, but a gentleman was politely detailed to
conduct me there and look up the letters. I opened my
Miss. Doc. 58 and pointed out the long list of letters of
Mr. Wade's, on pages 23, 24, 25, and 26, and asked to see
those first.

The gentlemen expressed his astonishment that, with
such a document in my hand, I should ask for *originals.*
He said that the documents printed by order of Congress
were to all intents and purposes the same as the originals,
as they were never so printed until those letters and papers
had been examined and proved to be genuine. I asked if
the printing was also a guarantee for Miss Carroll's papers
as printed in that document, though we were now unable
to find the originals. He replied assuredly it was ; that I
could positively rely upon all that had been so printed.

There was no going back upon the Congressional records. Other gentlemen came up and confirmed the statement.

Under these circumstances it seemed unneccessary to carry the investigation any further, so with thanks for the great friendliness and courtesy that I had met with I took up my precious Miss. Doc. 58 and departed with a slight intimation that if anything more should be needed they might have the pleasure of seeing me again.

The missing documents, after being on file for 8 years, were sent on one or more occasions from the War Department to the Capitol for examination by committees.

On page 30 of the Miss. Doc. 58 we learn the reason, on testimony of Wade and Hunt (keeper of the records), why they are there no longer.

———

For list of documents see pages 29 and 82.

On page 178 of the memorial of '78 Judge Evans, in one of the many repeated letters and statements of great interest that I have been obliged to omit for want of space, relates how he stood beside Miss Carroll in her parlor at St. Louis when she was gathering the information for the preparation of her paper to the War Department of November 30, 1861, and its accompanying map. He says, " I have a very distinct recollection of aiding her in the preparation of that paper, tracing with her upon a map of the United States, which hung in her parlor, the Memphis and Charleston railroad and its connections southward, the course of the Tennessee, the Alabama, and the Tombigbee rivers, and the position of Mobile Bay ; and when Henry fell she wrote the Department, showing the feasability of going either to Mobile or Vicksburg."

In his testimony given on page 85 of Miss. Doc. 179, he says, " On Miss Carroll's return from the West she prepared and submitted to the deponent, for his opinion, the plan of the Tennessee river expedition, as set forth in her memorial. Being a native and resident of that part of the section and intimately acquainted with its geography, and particularly with the Tennessee river, deponent was convinced of the vast military importance of her paper, and advised her to lose no time in laying the same before the War Department,

(XIV)

which she did on or about November 30, 1861. The accompanying map, rapidly prepared by Miss Carroll, was made on ordinary writing paper. An unpretentious map, but fraught with immense importance to the national cause.

Assistant Secretary of War Thomas A. Scott, the great railroad magnate and a man of remarkably acute mind, saw at a glance the immense importance of the plan ; he hastened with it to Lincoln, and when her plan of campaign was determined on he studied her map with the greatest care before going West to consolidate the troops for the coming campaign.

The second map sent in with Miss Carroll's paper of October, 1862, when the army before Vicksburg was meeting with disastrous failure, was made on regular map paper, representing the fortifications at Vicksburg, demonstrating that they could not be taken on the plan then adopted and indicating the right course to pursue. Miss Carroll bought the paper for the map at Shillington's, corner of Four-and-a-Half street and Pennsylvania avenue ; sketched it out herself with blue and red pencils and ink and took it to the War Department.

On page 24 of Miss. Doc. 58, Judge Wade writes :

" Referring to a conversation with Judge Evans last evening he called my attention to Colonel Scott's telegram announcing the fall of Island No. 10 in 1862 as endorsing your plan, when Scott said, ' the movement in the rear has done the work.' I stated to the Judge, as you and he knew before, that your paper on the reduction of Vicksburg had done the work on that place, after being so long baffled and with the loss of so much life and treasure by trying to take it from the water; that to my knowledge your paper was approved and adopted by the Secretary of War and immediately sent out to the proper military authority in that Department."

On April 16, 1891, by permission of the kindly authorities of the War Department, search was made in the office of the Chief Engineer to see if, by chance, these maps might have come to the War Department. No trace or record was found and it seemed to be agreed that, considering the circumstances of extreme secrecy attending the inauguration of the campaign, it was unlikely that they should come there. Time, which so often coroborates the truth, may possibly bring those maps to light. At present I cannot trace them.

———

It is proposed to follow this volume with another, entitled " Civil War Papers in Aid of the Administration," by Anna Ella Carroll, with notes by the author.

CHAPTER I.

In looking at the map of Maryland we find that the configuration of the State is of an unusual character. The eastern portion is divided through the middle by the broad waters of Chesapeake Bay, leaving nine counties with the State of Delaware on the long stretch between the Chesapeake, Delaware Bay, and the Atlantic Ocean. Of late years the great tide of population has set toward the western side of Chesapeake Bay, leaving the widely divided eastern counties in a comparatively quiet and primitive condition. But in the earlier history of our country these eastern counties, with easy access to the Atlantic Ocean, were of greater comparative importance to the State, and were a center of culture and of hospitality. It was in Somerset, one of the two southernmost of these eastern counties, that Sir Thomas King, coming from England about the middle of the eighteenth century, purchased an extensive domain.

Landing first in Virginia with a group of colonists, he there married Miss Reid, an English lady also highly connected and of an influential family. The estate which he subsequently purchased in Maryland embraced several plantations, extending from the county road back to a creek, a branch of the Annemessex river, then and since known as King's creek.

(1)

Standing well back and divided from the county road by extensive grounds, Sir Thomas King built Kingston Hall, a pleasant and commodious residence. An avenue of fine trees, principally Lombard poplars and the magnificent native tulip tree, formed the approach to the Hall, and its gardens were terraced down to the creek behind.

On one of the outlying plantations Sir Thomas King also established the little village of Kingston, of which he built and owned every house. He brought hither settlers, but the little place did not thrive. Plantation life and proprietary ownership were not conducive to the growth of cities. As the old settlers died out the houses were abandoned, and the post office was removed to a corner of the Hall plantation, then known as Kingston Corner. A new settlement grew up there, and since emancipation has changed the conditions of life it has grown and thriven. It is now a promising little place of 250 inhabitants. It has assumed to itself the name of the older village and is known as Kingston on the present maps.

At the Hall Sir Thomas King established his family residence. Here he lived and here his wife died, leaving but one child, a daughter, heiress to these wide estates, the future mother of Governor Thomas King Carroll and the grandmother of Anna Ella Carroll, whose interesting career is the subject of our present relation.

Through all the early history of Maryland the contests between Catholic and Protestant form one of its most conspicuous features. Early settled by Lord Baltimore, a Catholic proprietary, his followers were at once involved in a struggle with still earlier settlers at Kent Island, in the Chesapeake Bay, and the Protestants who followed, while condemning Catholicism as a rule of faith, associated it also with the doctrine of divine right and arbitrary rule. Bitter contests followed. The most active minds of the Colony enrolled themselves enthusiastically in the opposing parties.

St. Mary's, a little town on the western side of the Chesapeake, was the ancient capital of the State and the headquarters of Catholicism.

Sir Thomas King, on his side, was a staunch Presbyterian. This household was strictly ruled in conformity to his faith, and by liberal contribution and personal influence he was largely instrumental in building the first Presbyterian meeting-house, at the little town of Rehoboth, a few miles from his own domain, a great barn-like structure of red brick, which remains to this day. The marriage of Miss King with her cousin, young Mr. Armstead, of Virginia, the ward of Sir Thomas King, was an event that had been planned for in both families, and was looked forward to with great satisfaction on all sides.

One may well imagine, then, the consternation which ensued to the proprietor of the Hall, to his relatives and friends, and all the neighbors of that staunch Presbyterian region, when Colonel Henry James Carroll, of St. Mary's, of the old Catholic family of the noted Charles Carroll, and himself a Catholic by profession, came across the waters of the Chesapeake, courting the only daughter of Sir Thomas King, the heiress to all these estates and the reigning belle of the county.

In vain was the bitter opposition of father and friends. The willful young heiress insisted on giving to the handsome officer from St. Mary's the preference over all her other admirers. It may be that a reaction from the strict rules and the severe tenets of her education gave to this young scion of another faith an additional charm. However that may be, love won the day.

The father was compelled to yield, and the young heiress became the wife of the intrepid Colonel Henry James Carroll. It could hardly have been expected that Sir Thomas King should associate with himself under the same roof a son-in-law of principles so opposed to his own ; but he established the young couple on the adjacent estate of Bloomsborough, which he also owned, and here their little son, Thomas King Carroll, first saw the light of day.

The old proprietor, in his great empty hall, coveted this little grandson and proposed to adopt him as his own child and make him the heir to all his estates.

In course of time a younger son, Charles Cecilius Carroll, was born to the Bloomsborough household, the grandfather's proposition was accepted, and little Thomas King Carroll, then between five and six years of age, became an inmate of Kingston Hall and the object of Sir Thomas King's devoted affection and brightest hopes.

Governor Carroll, in after times, used to relate to his children how they spent the winter evenings alone in the old Hall. His grandfather, in his spacious armc-hair, on one side of the open hearth, with a blazing wood fire and tall brass andirons ; the little boy, in a low chair, on the

opposite side, listening to the tales that his grandfather related of ancient times and heroic deeds.   By these means
Sir Thomas King strove to amuse his youthful heir and to
train his mind to high principles and brave aspirations.
But Sunday must have been a terrible day to the little boy,
attending long services in the red brick meeting-house and
occupying himself as he best could between whiles with the
old English family Bible, with pictures of devils and lakes
of fire and brimstone, calculated to inspire his youthful
mind with horror and alarm.

At an early age the young heir was sent to college, to
the Pennsylvania University at Philadelphia, then the most
famous seat of learning for those parts.   Here he graduated
with distinguished honors, at the age of seventeen.   Among
his classmates and intimate friends were Mr. William M.
Meredith, of Philadelphia; Benjamin Gratz, of St. Louis,
and the father of Mr. Mitchell, the author of Ike Marvel.

Returning to Maryland, Thomas King Carroll began the
study of law with Ephraim King Wilson, who had been
named after Sir Thomas King.   He was the father of the
late United States Senator for Maryland.   His studies
being completed, arrangements were made to associate him
as partner with Robert Goodloe Harper, the son-in-law of
Charles Carroll, of Carrollton, in his lucrative law practice,
and a house was engaged for his future residence in Baltimore.

During the studies of Thomas King Carroll, his aged
grandfather, Sir Thomas King, having died, Colonel Henry
James Carroll and his family were residing at Kingston
Hall and managing the estate for the young heir.

An old friend of the family was Dr. Henry James Stevenson, one of the prominent physicians of Baltimore. Dr. Stevenson had come over formerly as a surgeon in the British army. He had married in England Miss Anne Henry, of Hampton. Settling in Baltimore, he acquired a large estate, then on the outskirts, now in the center of Baltimore. On Parnassus Hill he built a very spacious and handsome residence. During the Revolutionary War Dr. Stevenson remained loyal to his British training and was an outspoken Tory. The populace of Baltimore were so incensed against him that they mobbed his residence, threatening to destroy it. The Doctor showed his military courage by standing, fully armed, in his doorway and threatening to shoot the first man who attempted to enter. The mob were so impressed by his determined attitude that they finally retired, leaving the owner and his property uninjured. Dr. Stevenson afterwards became much beloved through his devotion and care, bestowed alike on the wounded of both armies. He became noted in the profession from his controversy with Dr. Benjamin Rush, of Philadelphia, the one advocating and the other opposing inoculation for small-pox. Dr. Stevenson was so enthusiastic that he gave up, temporarily, his beautiful residence as a hospital for the support of his theory.

An ivory miniature in a gold locket, now in possession of Miss Carroll, represents Dr. Stevenson in his red coat and white waistcoat, and at the back of the locket there is a picture of Parnassus Hill, crowned by the Doctor's residence, with a perpendicular avenue straight up hill, and a negro attendant opening the gate at the foot for Dr. Stevenson, mounted on his horse and returning home. It is a very quaint and valuable specimen of ante-revolutionary art.

The daughter of this valiant doctor was a beautiful and accomplished girl, Miss Juliana Stevenson. She is described as having very regular features, a complexion of dazzling fairness, deep blue eyes, and auburn hair flowing in curls upon her shoulders. She was a good musician, playing the organ at her church, and educated carefully in every respect. Her knowledge of English history was considered something phenomenal.

Thomas King Carroll early won the affections of this lovely girl, and they were married by Bishop Kemp before the youthful bridegroom had completed his twentieth year.

Those that care for heraldry may be interested to know that at Baltimore may be seen the eight coats-of-arms belonging to the King-Carroll family, of which Miss Anna Ella is the eldest representative.

When the question came of Miss Stevenson leaving home, her especial attendant, a bright colored woman, had been given her choice of remaining with Dr. Stevenson's family or accompanying her mistress. The poor woman was greatly exercised in choosing between conflicting ties.

Mrs. Carroll was accustomed to describe to her children, with much feeling, the scene which followed. Sitting in her room she heard a knock at the door and in rushed Milly, with her face bathed in tears, and throwing herself at Miss Stevenson's feet she exclaimed " Oh, mistis, I can-

not, cannot, leave you !'' It was a moment of deep emotion
for both mistress and maid. Milly followed Mrs. Carroll
to her new home and became the old mammy, the dear old
mammy of all the Carroll children.

Her daughter Leah was born on the Kingston plantation,
and then her grandaughter Milly, who in later times clung
to the changing fortunes of the Carroll family, and is at
this day a devoted attendant on her invalid mistress, Miss
Anna Ella Carroll. A visitor to the modest home in Washington, now occupied by the Carroll sisters, is met at the
door by the comely face and pleasant smile of this same
faithful Milly. The life-long devotion of the affectionate
'' Mammy '' illustrates one of the most touching features
of the old plantation life ; but the shadow of slavery was
over it all. To follow the fortunes of her adored mistress,
Mammy left behind her in Baltimore her husband, a free
colored man. But what was the marital relation to a slave !
The youthful couple set out on a wedding tour, but were un-
expectedly recalled by the sudden death of Colonel Henry
James Carroll. It was necessary for his son to return at
once and take possession his of inheritance.

The coming home of the proprietor and his youthful
bride was a great event at Kingston Hall. There were at
that time on the plantation 150 slaves, besides the children.
They are described as a fine and stalwart people, looking
as if they belonged to a different race from the colored people that we now meet with in cities. They seemed like a
race of giants. The men were usually as much as six feet in
height, and broad and muscular in proportion. All these

numerous dependents were drawn up in lines on the long avenues, dressed in their livery of green and buff, and must have presented an imposing appearance as the stately family carriage was seen approaching through the long vista of fine old trees. The arrival was heralded by a roar of welcome and demonstrations of joy.

And thus the youthful couple took possession of the home that was to be the scene of so many joys and so many sorrows, ending in troublous times that completely changed the existing order of things, and which witnessed the conclusion of the reign of the Kings and the Carrolls at Kingston Hall.

Shortly after his return with his bride Thomas King Carroll was elected to serve in the Legislature. He only attained the requisite age of 21 years on the day before he took his seat. His birth-day was celebrated at Kingston Hall after the old English fashion, and he was fêted and toasted and received congratulations on all sides. It is said that he was the youngest member ever elected to the Legislature.

Thomas King Carroll commenced life not only with wide social advantages, but with great natural gifts. He was striking in appearance, and of so graceful and dignified a demeanor that it is said that he never entered a crowd without a movement of respect and appreciation showing the impression that he created.

He was a good orator and of unimpeachable integrity and lofty character. This was early exemplified when as still very youthful he was sent to represent his county at a po-

litical caucus in Baltimore. The question of raising money
for the approaching campaign came up, and he was asked
in his turn how much would be needed for his county of
Somerset. He arose and said: "With all due deference,
Mr. President, *not one cent.* We can carry our county without any such aid!" There was a general laugh, and Robert Goodloe Harper, who was present, said, "Very well,
young gentleman, you will tell a different tale a few years
hence." He went home and related the proceedings to his
constituents, who applauded his answer, and that year
Somerset was the banner county of the State.

The early years succeeding the marriage were years of
peace and prosperity.

The young bride won all hearts by her beauty and the
sweetness of her disposition.

In time a lively group of children filled the old Hall
with life and gayety.

Thomas King Carroll, like many another Maryland
planter, was fully convinced that in itself slavery was
wrong. The early settlers of Maryland would gladly have
excluded it, but the institution was forced upon them by
the mother country, the English monarch and his court
deriving large incomes from the sale of slaves and canceling
every law made by the early settlers to prevent their introduction into the colony. Slavery had now become a
settled institution, on which the whole social fabric was built,
and individual proprietors, however they might disapprove
of the system, could see no way to change it. All that
Thomas King Carroll knew how to do was to seek as far as

possible the happiness and **welfare of** his slaves, and slavery showed itself on the Kingston plantation in its mildest and most attractive form.

Not much money was made usually upon plantations, but everything was produced upon the estate that was needed to feed and clothe the great group of dependents. And this was the state of things at Kingston **Hall.**

There was Uncle Nathan, the butler, whose wife was Aunt Susan, the dairywoman ; Uncle Davy, the shoemaker ; Saul, the blacksmith ; Mingo, the old body servant of Colonel Carroll ; Fortune, the coachman, etc., etc.—all very powerful men.

Every trade was represented upon the estate. There were blacksmith shops ; there were shoemakers, tanners, weavers, dyers, etc. All the goods worn by the servants, male and female, were manufactured on the place. The wool was sheared from the sheep, and went through every process needed to produce the linsey-woolsey garments of men and women. The women were allowed to choose the colors of their dresses, and the wool was dyed in accordance with their tastes. Two of these dresses were allowed for a winter's wear, and each woman was furnished with a new calico print for Sundays.

There were few local preachers among them at that time, but two were noticeable during the childhood of the Carroll children, Ethan Howard and Uncle Saul. And there was an Uncle Remus, too, in Fortune, the coachman, who told the children the stories of Brer Rabbit and the Tar-baby quite as effectively as the Uncle Remus of our popular magazines.

The servants had their own rivalries and class distinctions. One portion of the house servants prided themselves as being the old servants—born on the place. Another group plumed themselves as having come in with the " Mistis," and having seen outside regions and a wider range of life. But all the house servants considered themselves vastly superior to the field hands and treated them with condescension.

The house servants, though slaves, in fact, were absolute despots in their own department. The Carroll children would not have dared to touch a knife or a fork without the permission of the butler, and if they had attempted to enter the cellar or the dairy without leave from their respective guardians a revolutionary war would have been the result.

Mammy, too, was the absolute ruler over every shoe and stocking, and was expected under all circumstances to be responsible for every article of the children's toilet.

The largest quarter devoted to the slaves was a great circular structure, with a central hall surrounded by partitions, giving to each field hand a separate sleeping birth. The hall in the center was devoted to those who were old or unfitted for work, and here the young children were deposited while their parents were pursuing their tasks, and they were expected to wait upon the " Grannies " and be cared for in return.

Behind this central apartment was one in which the food was prepared, and there was a great hand-mill, where the corn was ground for the daily use.

The children at the Hall were seldom allowed to enter these quarters, but were occasionally granted permission to go there when delicacies for the sick or new caps and dresses for the babies were furnished from the Hall.

There were also quarters for the married slaves, each family having its little cottage and garden, which it was allowed to cultivate on its own account, and great was the pride of its occupants if by dint of especial care they could raise the spring vegetables earlier than in the master's garden, and carry them up to the Hall in triumph. There they always found a customer ready to purchase their produce. Every Monday morning rations were given out for a week by the overseer and they were cooked by the families in their own quarters.

The hours of work were moderate, and on Saturday they had a half holiday.

Sometimes there were parties and merry-makings at the negro quarters. On great occasions, such as the marriage of a house servant, the family at the Hall, by their presence, gave dignity to the festivities, and inwardly they greatly enjoyed the fantastic scene.

At Kingston Hall open house was kept, and numerous visitors and entertainments made life gay for the children, who grew up in an atmosphere of ease and hospitality, little anticipating the vicissitudes of the future and the stormy and heart-rending times in which their country was about to be involved.

CHAPTER II.

On August the 29th, 1815, Anna Ella Carroll was born, at Kingston Hall. By this time a little brick Episcopal church had also been built at Rehoboth, but the congregation was too small to support a resident clergyman, and it had to alternate with other churches in its services. At this infant church, in due course of time, Anna Ella was christened by the Rev. Mr. Slemmonds. She was the eldest child, and thenceforth the pride of her distinguished father, who viewed with delight her remarkable intelligence, and early made her his companion in the political interests in which he took such an active part. It soon became evident that this was a child of decided and unusual character. When but three years old she would sit on a little stool at her father's feet, in his library, listening intently as he read aloud his favorite passages from Shakespeare.

All Mr. Carroll's children were so drilled in Shakespeare that there was not one of them who could not, when some-

KINGSTON HALL.—BIRTH PLACE OF ANNA ELLA CARROLL.

what older, repeat long passages by rote, and they made the rehearsal of scenes from Shakespeare's plays one of their favorite amusements.   Anna Ella showed no taste for accomplishments; cared neither for dancing, drawing, music, or needlework.   She used to boast to her sisters that she had made a shirt beautifully when ten years old; but they would smile at the idea, as they had never seen her handle a needle and could associate her only with books.

These were to her of absorbing interest, and books, too, of a grave and thoughtful character.   Alison's History and Kant's Philosophy were her favorite reading at eleven years of age.   She read fiction to some extent, under her father's direction; but, with the exception of Shakespeare and Scott, she never cared for it.   While other girls of her age were entranced by Sir Charles Grandison and fascinated by the heroes of Bulwer's earlier novels, she turned from them to read Coke and Blackstone with her father, and followed with him the political debates and discussions of the day.   She studied with lively interest the principles and events which led to the separation of the Colonists from the Mother Country, and buried herself in theological questions.   At a very early age her letters bore reference to the gravest subjects.   Imagination was never prominent; her mind was essentially analytical.   Pure reason and clear consecutive argument delighted her, and works of that nature were eagerly sought by her.

Her life passed largely in her father's excellent library, which was well stocked with classic works, both history, biography, philosophy, and poetry, and her education was to him a constant delight.

Miss Carroll's early associates were the children of the neighboring proprietors, the Handys, the Wilsons, the Gales, the Henrys, etc., and she early made acquaintance with the distinguished men who where her father's associates.

Mr. Carroll continued to serve in the Legislature until elected Governor of Maryland, in 1829. On this occasion he received an interesting letter from Charles Carroll, of Carrollton, congratulating him and expressing his pride and gratification at the event. When Governor Thomas King Carroll went to Annapolis, in performance of the duties of his office, he was accompanied by Mrs. Carroll, with the younger children and a group of servants under the superintendence of the invaluable Mammy. Mrs. Carroll, by her beauty and accomplishments, was well fitted to adorn her station. When the weather became warm she returned with her children to Kingston Hall.

The following charming letters from Miss Carroll, then a girl of fourteen, show the tenderness of the relation between father and child, and at how early an age she interested herself in politics and entered into the questions of the day :

KINGSTON HALL, *Jan. 20, 1830.*

MY PRECIOUS FATHER :

My dearest mother received your letter on Monday, and we were all happy to know you had arrived safely at the seat of government, although the Annapolis paper had previously announced it.

Oh ! my dear father, if I could but see you ! I miss you—

we all miss you—beyond measure. The time passes tediously without you.

I have just read Governor Martin's last message.* I think it quite well written. I wondered to see it published in the *Telegraph* [an opposition paper, I suppose]. I am anxious to see what the Eastern papers say of your election. Please, dear father, when anything relating to your political action is published, whether in the form of a message, in pamphlet, or in newspaper, do not fail to let us have them. I read with so much pride your letter in the Annapolis paper. It merits all the distinction and fame it has brought you. Too much could not be said in praise of my noble father. Dr. K—— was here to-day. He says they feel "quite exalted" to be so near neighbors to a Governor.

When do you think the Legislature will rise? But I must not write on political subjects only. Brother is delighted with his new horse. The little children are begging dearest mother to write you for them. May every blessing attend you, my precious father. Be sure and write me a *long* letter.

Your devoted daughter,

A. E. CARROLL.

KINGSTON HALL, *Feb. 17, 1830.*

MY BELOVED FATHER:

Again we are disappointed in your arrival home! *and how* disappointed no tongue can tell. Dearest mother thought it possible you might come on a little visit, even if the Legislature did not rise. † You said in your last letter to me that this was "probable." Why did you not say

---

* He was Governor Carroll's predecessor.

† At that time the sessions of the Legislature were not restricted, as now they are, to sixty days.

2 C

"*certain?*" Then I would rejoice, for when my father says
a thing is certain, I *know* it is certain. I am happy to tell
you that I am much better; have had a long and tedious
spell. I would lie for hours and think of you away from
me, and if I had not the kindest and tenderest mother to
care for me and for us all, what should we do. I understand that your appointments have not been generally approved by the milk-and-water strata of the party, of course,
for no thorough Jackson man would denounce, even if he did
not approve. It is my principle, as well as that of Lycur-
gus, to avoid "mediums"—that is to say, people who are
not decidedly one thing or the other. In politics they are
the inveterate enemies of the State. I hear there has been
a committee appointed to visit you on your return to the
Hall and present a petition for the removal of some whom
you have recently appointed. They call themselves reform-
ers. I want reform, too, even in court criers, but to be forever reforming reform is absurd. I know whatever you
do is *right*, and needs no reform, my wisest and dearest of
fathers.

Write as soon as you can to your loving child,

A. E. CARROLL.

Mrs. Carroll was a devoted member of the Church of
England, as was natural in the daughter of staunch Dr.
Stevenson.

As there were no Sunday schools in those days, Mrs.
Carroll gathered her children around her on Sunday after-
noons and drilled them in the church catechism until it was
as familiar to them as their A B C; but Anna Ella always
inclined to the Westminster Confession and the tenets in
which her father's childhood had been so rigorously educated.

When about fifteen Miss Carroll was sent to a boarding school, at West River, near Annapolis, to pursue her studies with Miss Margaret Mercer, an accomplished teacher.

Thomas King Carroll, at the same age, had been sent to the University of Pennsylvania, and afterward to the law school; but for this girl of gifts so remarkable, and of a character so decided, the best thing that the world of those times offered was a young ladies' boarding school of the olden time. Well it was for her and her country that her exceptional position as the cherished daughter of a man of such education and talent, occupied with political affairs, secured for her an education that would otherwise have been unattainable to her.

However, she made the best possible use of such education as a ladylike school permitted, was noted for her intelligence, and made many friends; but her true education began and continued with Governor Carroll at home.

Miss Carroll had early shown an intense interest in moral and religious questions, following her father's views on these subjects. She became interested in the ministrations of Dr. Robert J. Breckenridge, of Kentucky, then settled over a Presbyterian church in Baltimore.

Dr. Breckenridge was the uncle of John C. Breckenridge, afterward one of the leading secessionists, utterly opposed to his uncle in political views, and one of the candidates for the Presidency in 1860.

Dr. Robert J. Breckenridge was a valued friend of Governor Carroll.

Miss Anna Ella became a communicant and earnest

member of his church, and a mutual friendship arose, terminated only by the death of the aged minister, who has left on record his high appreciation of the mental abilities and the great services afterward rendered by his remarkable parishioner.

We will give in part two letters from this excellent man to Miss Carroll, written from Kentucky in after years. For want of space we must greatly shorten them.

DANVILLE, KY., *December 6, 1864.*

MY EXCELLENT FRIEND :

It is very seldom I have read a letter with more gratification than yours of November 29th. How kind it is of you, after so many events, to remember me ; and how many people and events and trials and enjoyments, connected with years of labor, rush through my heart and my brain as you recall Maryland and Baltimore so freshly and suddenly to me ; and how noble is the picture of a fine life, well spent, which the modest detail of some of your efforts realizes to me. It is no extravagance, not even a trace of romance ; it is a true enjoyment, and deeply affecting, too, that you give me in what you recount and what is recalled thereby. For what is there in our advanced life more worthy of thankfulness to God than that our former years were such that if we remember them with tears they are tears of which we need not be ashamed. My life during the almost twenty years since I left Maryland has been, as the preceding period had all been, a scene of unremitting effort in very many ways ; and now, if the force of invincible habit permitted me to live otherwise, I should hardly escape by any other means a solitary if not a desolate old age. Solitary, because of a numerous family all, except one young son, are either in the great battle of life or in their graves. Desolate, because the terrible curse which marks our times and desolates our country has divided my house, like thousands of others, and my children literally fight in opposite armies and my kindred and friends die by each other's hands. There is no likelihood, in my opinion, that our Legislature will send me to the Senate of the United States; and will you wonder if I assure you that I have never desired that they should. Was it not a purer, perhaps a higher, ambition to prove that in the most frightful times and through long years a simple citizen had it in his power by his example, his voice and his pen, by courage, by disinterestedness, by toil, to become a real power in the State of himself; and have not you, delicately nurtured woman as you are, also cherished a similar ambition and done a similar work, even from a more difficult position? * * * I beg to be remembered in kind terms to your father, and that you will accept the assurances of my great respect and esteem.

ROBERT J. BRECKENRIDGE.

DANVILLE, KY., April 27, 1865.

MY DEAR MISS CARROLL :

* * * You will easily understand how much I value the good opinion you express of my past efforts to serve our country, and of my ability to serve it still further ; and it is very kind of you to report to me with your approbation the good opinion of others, whom to have satisfied is in a measure fame. * * * Many years ago, without reserve and with a perfect and irrevocable consecration, I gave myself and all I had to Him, and have never, for one moment, regretted that I did so. The single principle of my existence, from that day to this, has been to do with my might what it was given to me to see it was God's will

I should do. You see, my dear Miss Carroll, that I, who never sought anything, am not now capable of seeking anything, nor even permitted to do so ; and, on the other hand, that I, who never refused to undertake any duty, am not allowed now to hesitate, if the Lord shows me the way, nor permitted to refuse what my country might demand of me. This is all I can say—all I have cared to say for nearly my whole life. I would not turn my hand over to secure any earthly power or distinction. I would not hesitate a moment to lay down my life to please God or to bless my country.

Mr. Lincoln was my personal friend and habitually expressed sentiments to me which did me the highest honor.

It gives me pleasure to learn that you propose to publish annals of this revolution, and I trust you will be spared to execute your purpose.

Make my cordial salutations to your father and accept the assurance of my high respect and esteem.

Your friend, &c.,

R. J. BRECKENRIDGE.

Miss Carroll was very pleasing, with a fine and intelligent face, an animated and cordial manner, and great life and vivacity, roused into fire and enthusiasm on any topic that appealed to her intellect and her sympathies. Naturally, in so favorable a social position and with such gifts, she received early in life much attention and had offers of marriage from many distinguished parties ; but she never seemed inclined to change her condition or to give up the beloved companionship of her father. A literary life and his congenial presence seemed to be all-sufficient for her, and she remained his devoted companion until his death, in

1873, when she also, the child of his youth, was well advanced in life.

After Governor Carroll's term of office had expired he returned to his estate, and shortly after he was waited upon by a deputation, who had been sent to enquire if he would accept a nomination as United States Senator. But at that time Mrs. Carroll was dangerously ill. His extensive plantation and group of children required his presence, and he declined to serve. He was devoted to his wife, and their marriage was one of unbroken harmony until her death, in 1849. Governor Carroll devoted himself thereafter to the necessities of his family and estate.

Anna Ella Carroll frequently visited her friends at Washington, and early commenced an extended relation with the press, writing usually anonymously on the political subjects of the day. A friend of her father, Thomas Hicks, considered that he owed his election as Governor of Maryland largely to the articles which she contributed in his favor, and he retained through life a strong personal friendship and high admiration for her intellectual powers. At his death he left her his papers and letters, to be edited by her—a labor prevented by her subsequent illness. In 1857 Miss Carroll published a considerable work, entitled " The Great American Battle,'' or Political Romanism, that being the subject of immediate discussion at that time. This work was compiled from a series of letters contributed by her to the press, and her family knew nothing of the project until she surprised them by the presentation of the bound volume.

Old Sir Thomas King would certainly have been greatly gratified if he could have known how vigorously his great-granddaughter was to uphold the banner of religious and political freedom.   This work was accompanied by an excellent portrait of the authoress in the prime of life, which we here reproduce for our present readers.

In the following year Miss Carroll published another considerable work, entitled " The Star of the West," relating to the exploration of our Western Territories, their characteristics, the origin of the National claims, and our duties towards our new acquisitions, and she urged the building of the Pacific railroad.   This seems to have been one of her most popular works, as it went through several editions, and greatly extended her acquaintance with leading men.

The following letter, written by the Hon. Edward Bates, is very descriptive of Miss Carroll and evinces the admiration and esteem which she inspired among those best fitted to appreciate her high character, her uncommon cultivation, and natural gifts.

WASHINGTON, D. C., *October 3, 1863.*

To Hon. ISAAC HAZLEHURST, *of Philadelphia.*

MY DEAR SIR: I have just received a note from Miss Anna Ella Carroll, of Maryland, informing me she is going to Philadelphia, where she is a comparative stranger, and desiring an introduction to some of the eminent publicists of your famous city.

I venture to present her to you, sir, first, as an unquestionable lady of the highest personal standing and family connection ; second, as a person of superior mind, highly cultivated, especially in the solids of American literature, political history, and constitutional law ; third, of strong will, indomitable courage, and patient labor. Guided by the light of her own understanding, she seeks truth among the mixed materials of other minds, and having found it, maintains it against all obstacles ; fourth and last, a writer fluent, cogent, and abounding with evidence of patient investigation and original thought.

I commend her to your courtesy, less for the delicate attentions proper for the drawing room than for the higher communion of congenial students, alike devoted to the good of the Commonwealth.

With the greatest respect, I remain, sir, your friend and servant.

Edward Bates.

As time went on, Thomas King Carroll, now advanced in years, many of his children married and scattered, began to find his estate and great group of dependents a burdensome and unprofitable possession.

Under a humane master, unwilling to sell his slaves, they were apt to increase beyond the resources of the plantation to sustain them. Ready-money payment was not the general rule upon plantations. Abundance of food was produced, but money was not very pientiful when markets were distant and trade very limited.

It was not unusual for debts to accumulate and even to be handed down from father to son. The creditors rather favored this state of things, as the debt drew interest. As long as there were plenty of slaves, their ultimate payment was secure whenever they chose to press for it. If the money was not then forthcoming, their redress was certain— a descent followed of that brutal intermediary, " the nigger dealer," loathed and dreaded alike by master and servant. A sufficient amount of the human property was speedily secured and driven off for sale to satisfy the creditor. To the slave, torn from his home and his life-long ties, it was despair. To the master's family, often a bitter grief. They might shut themselves up and weep at the outrage, but they were powerless in the face of an inexorable system. To the master, therefore, as the slaves increased, there could often be no alternative between ruthless sale and financial ruin. Thomas King Carroll, honorable, humane, unwilling to sell his slaves, immersed during the best years of his life in political affairs, found in later years his burdens increasing, and his kindness of heart had involved him also in some especial difficulties. He had on several occasions allowed his name to be used as security for friends in difficulty. Two or three of these debts remained un- paid and the responsibility came upon him. One especially, of an unusually large amount, involved him in embarrass- ment which led him to determine on the sale of his planta- tion. A neighbor and intimate friend, Mr. Dennis, was desirous to purchase, and very sorrowfully Thomas King Carroll came to the resolution to give up his ancestral home. As he was accustomed to say, he loved every corner and every stone upon the place, but the burden had become too great for his declining strength.

The sale was effected and Mr. Carroll removed to Dorchester county, on the eastern side of the Chesapeake, with his unmarried children, and here he died, in 1873, in his 80th year.

Governor Carroll is described in the annals of the State as "one of the best men Maryland has ever produced," a man of *character unsullied* and of lofty integrity.

At the breaking out of the civil war Mr. Carroll was already an elderly man. At first his sympathies were with his own section, but after the attack on Fort Sumter they were steadily enlisted for the National cause, though he foresaw that its triumph would lead to the destruction of his own fortunes and those of his children.

Most of the slaves had been left on the plantation, but some had always been considered the especial property of each of his children.

Thus Anna Ella Carroll had her own group. At the very outset of the war she fully realized that slavery was at the root of the rebellion, and she at once liberated her own slaves and devoted her time, her pen, and all her resources to the maintenance of the National cause. She immediately commenced a series of writings of such marked ability that they speedily attracted the attention of Mr. Lincoln and the Administration. Governor Hicks, too, placed in a situation of unusual difficulty, turned to his able friend for consultation and for moral and literary support.

Jefferson Davis, who was aware of Miss Carroll's great literary and social influence, wrote to her early in the secession movement adjuring her to induce her father to take sides with the South.

"I will give him any position he asks for," wrote Mr. Davis.

"Not if you will give him the whole South," replied Miss Carroll.

A visitor to her in 1861 says: "Her room was lined with military maps, her tables covered with papers and war documents. She would talk of nothing but the war. Her countenance would light up most radiantly as she spoke of the Union victories and the certainty that the great Nation must win an ultimate success."

When fresh news from the army came in she would step up to one of her charts and, placing a finger on a point, she would say: "Here is General ——'s detachment; here is the rebel army; such and such are the fortifications and surrounding circumstances; and she would then begin thoughtfully to predicate the result and suggest the proper move."

We will give a sketch of the situation in the early days of the secession movement, mainly in the words of Miss Carroll's own able account, afterwards published by order of Congress.

*List of Documents in Relation to Services Rendered by **Anna Ella Carroll**, to be Found in the Descriptive Catalogue of the Congressional Library.*

(Descriptive Catalogue, page 911.)

Petition for compensation for services. Anna Ella Carroll. March 31, 1870. Senate Mis. Doc. No. 100, 41st Congress, 2d session.

(Catalogue, page 928.)

Report on memorial of Miss Carroll. Senator Howard. February 2, 1871. Senate report No. 339, 41st Congress, 3d session.

(Catalogue, page 962.)

Memorial for payment of services. June 8, 1872. Senate Mis. Doc. No. 167, 42d Congress, 2d session, vol. II.

(Catalogue, page 1058.)

Petition for compensation for services. Anna Ella Carroll. February 14, 1876. House Mis. Doc. No. 179, 44th Congress, 1st session, vol. IX.

(Catalogue, **page** 1099.)

Memorial of Anna Ella Carroll. October 22, 1877. Senate Mis. Doc. No. 5, 45th Congress, 1st session, vol. I.

(Catalogue, page 1128.)

House of Representatives. Mis. Doc. No. 58, 45th Congress, 2d session. Claim of Anna Ella Carroll. Memorial of Anna Ella Carroll, of Maryland, praying for compensation for services rendered to the United States during the late civil war. May 18, 1878.

(Catalogue, page 1149.)

Report on claim of Anna Ella Carroll. Senator Cockrell February 18, 1879. Senate Report No. 775, 45th Congress, 3d session, vol. II.

(Catalogue, page 1241.)

Report of claim of Anna Ella Carroll. Representative E. S Bragg. March 3, 1881. House report No. 386, 46th Congress, 3d session, vol. II.

NOTE.—Most of these only to be seen by consulting the bound volumes in the Congressional Library.

(All the following letters, reports, etc., concerning Miss Carroll's literary and military services are reproduced from these Congressional documents.)

CHAPTER III.

"On the election of Mr. Lincoln, in 1860, the safety of the Union was felt to be in peril and its perpetuity to depend on the action of the border slave States, and, from her geographical position, especially on Maryland.

In the cotton States the Breckenridge party had conducted the canvass on the avowed position that the election of a sectional President—as they were pleased to characterize Mr. Lincoln—would be a virtual dissolution of the " compact of the Union ;" whereupon it would become the duty of all the Southern States to assemble in " sovereign convention " for the purpose of considering the question of their separate independence.

In Maryland the Breckenridge electors assumed the same position, and as the Legislature was under the control of that party, it was understood that could it assemble they would at once provide for a convention for the purpose of formally withdrawing from the Union. The sessions, however, were biennial, and could only be convened by authority of the Governor. It therefore seemed for the time that the salvation of the Union was in the hands of

(31)

Governor Hicks. Although he had opposed the election of
Mr. Lincoln and all his sympathies were on the side of
slavery, his strong point was devotion to the Union. With
this conviction, founded upon long established friendship,
Miss Carroll believed she might render some service to her
country, and took her stand with him at once for the
preservation of the Union, come weal or woe to the institution of slavery.

Governor Hicks had been elected some three years before as the candidate of the American party, and to the
publications Miss Carroll had contributed to that canvass
he largely attributed his election. It was therefore natural that when entering on the fierce struggle for the preservation of the Union, with the political and social powers
of the State arrayed against him, that he should desire whatever aid it might be in her power to render him.

A few days after the Presidential election Miss Carroll
wrote Governor Hicks upon the probable designs of the
Southern leaders should the cotton States secede, and suggested the importance of not allowing a call for the Legislature to be made a question. That she might be in a
position to make her services more effective, she repaired
to Washington on the meeting of Congress in December,
and soon understood that the Southern leaders regarded the
dissolution of the Union as accomplished.

The leading disunionists from Maryland and Virginia
were on the ground in consultation with the secession leaders in Congress, and the emissaries from the cotton States
soon made their appearance, when it was resolved to make

Maryland the base of their operations and bring her into the line of the seceding States before the power of the Democratic party had passed away, on the 4th of March, 1861.

Hence every agency that wickedness could invent was industriously manufacturing public opinion in Baltimore and all parts of the State to coerce Governor Hicks to convene the Legislature.

With Maryland out of the Union they expected to inaugurate their Southern Confederacy in the Capitol of the United States on the expiration of President Buchanan's term, on the 4th of March, and by divesting the North of the seat of Government and retaining possession of the public buildings and archives, they calculated with great confidence upon recognition of national independence by European powers. About the middle of December Miss Carroll communicated to Governor Hicks their designs on Maryland and suggested the propriety of a public announcement of his unalterable determination to hold Maryland to the Union.

After his address on the 3d of January, 1861, resolutions and letters from men and women endorsing his cause were received from Maryland and from all quarters of the United States.

Governor Hicks at that time was willing to abide by any terms of settlement that would save a conflict between the sections. He favored the compromise proposed by the border States committee, that slavery should not be forbidden, either by Federal or territorial legislation, south of

3 C

36° 30', and he was strongly inclined to base his action on the acceptance or rejection of the Crittenden resolutions by Congress.

On the 19th of January, 1861, he urged Miss Carroll to exert whatever influence she was able to induce Congress to adopt some measure of pacification ; but she was soon satisfied that no compromise that Congress would adopt would be accepted by the cotton States, and, perceiving the danger should the Governor commit himself to any impossible condition, informed him on the 24th of January that the Crittenden proposition would by no possibility receive the sanction of Congress.

All efforts to move the steadfastness of the Governor having failed, the President of the Senate and Speaker of the House of Delegates issued their call to the people to act independently of him and elect delegates to a convention. This was a most daring and dangerous proceeding, and had the plan succeeded and a convention assembled they would immediately have deposed the Governor and passed an ordinance of secession. The Governor was powerless in such an emergency to defend the State against the revolutionary body, as the State militia were on their side and Mr. Buchanan had declared that the National Government could not coerce a sovereign State.

The gravity of the situation was appreciated by the Governor and the friends of the Union. Miss Carroll addressed articles through the press and wrote many letters to prepare the public mind in Maryland for the struggle. Fortunately the people (thus warned) failed to endorse this call ; conse-

quently the leading statesmen of the disunion party abandoned their cherished expectation of inaugurating their
Government in the National Capitol.

Many of the conspirators, however, still sought to seize
Washington and forcibly prevent the inauguration of the
President elect on the 4th of March. The military organi-
zations of the South were deemed sufficient for the enter-
prise, and a leader trained in the wars of Texas was solic-
ited to lead them. The more sagacious of their party,
however, discountenanced the mad scheme. They assured
Miss Carroll that no attempt would be made to seize the
Capitol and prevent the inauguration of Mr. Lincoln, so
long as Maryland remained in the Union.

The ruthless assault upon the Massachusetts troops in
Baltimore, as they were passing through on their way to
Washington, on the 19th of April, with the antecedent and
attendant circumstances, roused to the highest degree the
passions of all who sympathized with the secession movement, and the mob became for the time being the controlling force of that city. So largely in the ascendant
was it and so confident were the disunionists in consequence that they, without warrant of law, assumed the
responsibility of issuing a call for the Legislature of Maryland to convene in Baltimore. Governor Hicks, fearing
that the Legislature would respond to the call, and that if
it did it would yield to the predominant spirit, give voice
to the purpose of the mob, and adopt an act of secession,
resolved to forestall such action by convening that body
to meet at Frederick City, away from the violent and men-
acing demonstrations of Baltimore.

The Legislature thus assembled contained a number of leading members who were ready at once for unconditional secession. There were also others who, with them, would constitute a majority and would vote for the measure could they be sustained by public sentiment, but who were not prepared to give that support without that assurance. The field of conflict was, therefore, transferred from the halls of legislation to the State at large, and to the homes of their constituents, and there the battle raged during the summer of 1861. In that conflict of ideas Miss Carroll bore an earnest and prominent part, and the most distinguished men have given repeated evidence that her labors were largely instrumental in thwarting the secessionists and saving Maryland to the Union. The objective point of the labors of the disunion leaders was a formal act of secession, by which Maryland would become an integral portion of the Confederacy, not only affording moral and material aid to the Southern cause, but relieving the rebel armies in crossing the Potomac from the charge, which at that stage of the conflict the leaders were anxious to avoid, of ignoring their vaunted doctrine of State rights by invading the territory of sovereign States. With the usual arguments that were urged to fire the Southern heart and to reconcile the people to the extreme remedy of revolution, special prominence was given to what was stigmatized as the abitrary and unconstitutional acts of President Lincoln. To place the people in possession of the true theory of their institutions and to define and defend the war powers of the Government were the special purposes of Miss Carroll's labors during these eventful months.''

It would not be possible in the compass of this paper to set forth circumstantially all the important questions that arose in the progress of the war, in the discussion of which Miss Carroll took part; but it is proper to say that on every material issue, from the inception of the rebellion to the final reconstruction of the seceded States, she contributed through the newspapers, in pamphlet form, and by private correspondence to the discussion of important subjects. Governor Hicks bore the brunt of this terrible conflict, greatly aided by Miss Carroll's public and private support, and stimulated by such inspiring letters as the following:

WASHINGTON HOUSE,
WASHINGTON CITY, *Jan.* 16, 1861.

MY DEAR GOVERNOR:

I have for some days intended to write and express my cordial admiration and gratitude for the noble stand you have now taken in behalf of the Union by the public address issued on the 3d instant. An extended relation with the leading presses of the country has enabled me in a public and more efficient manner to testify to this and create a public opinion favorable to your course of patriotic action throughout the land. Many of the articles you have seen emanated from this source.

I feel it will be a gratification to you, in the high and sacred responsibilities which surround your position, to know from one who is incapable of flattering or deceiving you the opinion privately held in this metropolis concerning your whole course since the secession movement in the South was practically initiated.

With all the friends of the Union with whom I converse, without regard to section or party, your course elicits the most unbounded applause. I might add to this the evidences furnished from private correspondence, but you doubtless feel already the sympathy and moral support to be derived in this way. I am often asked if I think you *can* continue to stand firm under the frightful pressure brought to bear upon you. I answer, *yes ;* that my personal knowledge enables me to express the confident belief that nothing will ever induce you to surrender while the oath to support the Constitution of your country and the vow to fulfill the obligations of your God rest upon your soul.

As a daughter of Maryland, I am proud to have her destiny in the hands of one so worthy of her ancient great name ; one who will never betray the sacred trust imposed upon him. "When God is for us, no man can be against us," is the Christian's courage when the day of trial comes.

I shall continue to fight your battle to the end.

Your sincere friend,

A. E. CARROLL.

Well might Governor Hicks say to her again and again, as in a letter to her in 1863 : "Your moral and material support I shall never forget in that trying ordeal, such as no other man in this country ever went through."

A little further on, Governor Hicks writes as follows :

ANNAPOLIS, MD., *December 17, 1861.*

MY DEAR MISS CARROLL :

In the hurry and excitement incident to closing my official relations to the State of Maryland I cannot find fitting words to express my high sense of gratitude to you for the kind and feeling manner in which you express your approval of my whole term of service in doing all in my power to uphold the honor and dignity of the State; but especially do I thank you for the personal aid you rendered me in the last part of my arduous duties.

When all was dark and dreadful for Maryland's future, when the waves of secession were beating furiously upon your frail executive, borne down with private as well as public grief, you stood nobly by and watched the storm and skillfully helped to work the ship, until, thank God, helmsmen and crew were safe in port.

*   *   *   *   *   *

With great regard, I have the honor to be ever your obedient friend and servant.

T. H. HICKS.

Thus it was that, supported by Miss Carroll, this high-minded and sorely tried man held fast to the end. He went into the struggle a rich man, in a position of worldly honor and prosperity. He came out of it reduced in prosperity, having, like other faithful Southern Unionists, lost his worldly possessions in that great upheaval. Thenceforth he lived, and he died, comparatively a poor man, but one of the noble and faithful who had acted an immortal part in the salvation of his country. All honor to brave and true-hearted Governor Hicks of Maryland!

Thus by her powerful advocacy and influence Miss Carroll largely contributed to securing the State of Maryland to the Union and saving the National Capital, and her writings also had a great effect upon the border States. Besides her numerous letters and newspaper articles, she began writing and publishing, at her own expense, a remarkable series of war pamphlets, which speedily became an important element in the guidance of the country.

Senator John C. Breckenridge, in the July Congress of 1861, made a notable secession speech. Miss Carroll replied to this in a pamphlet containing such clear and powerful arguments that the War Department circulated a large edition, and requested her to write on other important points then being discussed with great diversity of opinion.

The following letters give some indication of the timely nature and value of the Breckenridge pamphlet:

MY DEAR MISS CARROLL:

Your refutation of the sophistries of Senator Breckenridge's speech is full and conclusive. I trust this reply may have an extended circulation at the present time, as I am sure its perusal by the people will do much to aid the cause of the Constitution and the Union.

CALEB B. SMITH.*

———

GLOBE OFFICE, *Aug. 8, 1861.*

DEAR MISS CARROLL:

Allow me to thank you for the privilege of reading your admirable review of Mr. Breckenridge's speech. I have enjoyed it greatly. Especially have I been struck with its very ingenious and just exposition of the constitutional

---

* Caleb B. Smith was Secretary of Interior in Mr. Lincoln's Cabinet and an old friend of Miss Carroll.

law bearing on the President, assailed by Mr. B., and with the very apt citation of Mr. Jefferson's opinion as to the necessity and propriety of disregarding mere legal punctilio when the source of all is in danger of destruction. The gradual development of the plot in the South to over-throw the Union is also exceedingly well depicted and with remarkable clearness. If spoken in the Senate your article would have been regarded by the country as a complete and masterly refutation of Mr. B.'s heresies. Though the peculiar position of the *Globe* might preclude the publication of the review, I am glad that it has not been denied to the editor of the *Globe* to enjoy what the *Globe* itself has not been privileged to contain.

I remain, with great respect, your obedient servant,

SAM'L T. WILLIAMS.*

September 21, 1861.

DEAR MISS CARROLL :

I have this moment, 11 o'clock Saturday night, finished reading your most admirable reply to the speech of Mr. Breckenridge ; and now, my dear lady, I have only time to thank you for taking the trouble to embody for the use of others so much sound constitutional doctrine and so many valuable historic facts in a form so compact and manageable. The President received a copy left for him and re-quested me to thank you cordially for your able support.

The delay was not voluntary on my part. For some time past my time and mind have been painfully engrossed by very urgent public duties, and my best affections stirred by the present condition of Missouri, my own neglected

---

*Samuel T. **Williams** was at that time chief editor of the *Globe* (the Congressional **Record of the** day) and son-in-law of Mr. Rives, the owner of the *Globe*.

and almost ruined State ; and this is the reason why I have been so long deprived of the pleasure and instruction of perusing your excellent pamphlet.

I remain, with great respect and regard, your friend and obedient servant,

EDWARD BATES.*

APPLEBY, Sept. 22, 1861.

MY DEAR MISS CARROLL :

I will thank you very much if you will send me a couple of hundred copies of your reply to Breckenridge, with bill of expenses for the same. I do not think it is right that you should furnish your publications gratis any longer. I told our friends in Baltimore last week that the Union State Committee must go to work and send your documents over the entire State if they expect to carry this election. Mr. Mayer and Mr. Fickey, of the committee, said they would make application to you immediately and pay for all you can supply.

No money can ever pay for what you have done for the State and the country in this terrible crisis, but I trust and believe the time will come when all will know the debt they owe you.

With great respect, your friend and obedient servant,

THOS. H. HICKS.

BALTIMORE, Oct. 2, 1861.

MISS CARROLL :

If you could let me have more of your last pamphlet in answer to Breckenridge, I could use them with great effect.

---

*Edward Bates was the Attorney General of Mr. Lincoln's Cabinet and an intimate friend of Miss Carroll.

I have distributed from my house on Camden street all the committee could furnish me. I set my son at the door with paper and pencil, and five hundred men called for it in one day. These are the bone and sinew of the city, wanting to know which army to enter. Please send as many as you can spare. They go like hot cakes.

Yours very respectfully,

JAMES TILGHMAN.

———

A. S. Diven, in the House of Representatives, January 22, 1862:

"She signs herself Anna Ella Carroll. I commend her answer on the doctrine of the war power to those who have been following that phantom and misleading the people, and I recommend it to another individual, a friend of mine, who gave a most learned disquisition on the writ of *habeas corpus* and against the power of the President to imprison men. He will find that answered. I am not surprised at this. The French Revolution discovered great political minds in some of the French women, and I am happy to see a like development in our women."

Judge Diven subsequently addressed the following letter to Miss Carroll:

WASHINGTON, *February 9, 1862.*

I thank you for the note of the 6th. Your pamphlet I have read with satisfaction, as I had your former publication. I have no desire to appear complimentary, but cannot forbear the expression of my admiration of your writings. There is a cogency in your argument that I have seldom met with. Such maturity of judicial learning with so comprehensive and concise a style of communication surprises me. Ladies have certainly seldom evinced ability as jurists—it may be because the profession was not their sphere—but you have satisfied me that at least one might have been a distinguished lawyer. Go on, madam, in aiding the cause to which you have devoted your talent; your country needs the labor of all her defenders. If the time will ever come when men will break away from passion and return to reason your labors will be appreciated; unless that time soon arrives, alas for this Republic; I have almost despaired of the wisdom of men. God's ways are mysterious, and my trust in Him is left me as a ground of hope.

I have the honor to be, madam, your obedient servant,

A. S. DIVEN.*

BALTIMORE, *May 9, 1874.*

MISS CARROLL:

After the Presidential election in 1860 a Union Association was formed in Baltimore and I was elected chairman, which position I held until the Union party was formed in Maryland in 1861, when Brantz Mayer was made chairman and I was appointed treasurer, and held the position until 1863. We commenced at once to circulate your publications and sent them broadcast over the entire State.

When we appealed to you, you furnished them most liberally, and to our surprise and the relief of our treasury you informed us you made no charge.

All were disposed to give your articles a careful perusal,

---

*A. S. Diven was Member of Congress from New York, a railroad man, and, I think, is still living.

and many instances came to my knowledge of the great positive good they effected in keeping men within the Union party when the first blow of secession had been struck.

FRED. FICKEY, JR.

May 15, 1862.

I have never read an abler or more conclusive paper than your war-power document in all my reading.   *   *   *

RICHARD S. COXE.*

WASHINGTON, *May 22, 1862.*

I most cheerfully indorse the papers respecting your publications under the authority of the War Department. Mr. Richard S. Coxe, I can say, is one of the ablest lawyers in this District or in the country. In his opinion of your writings I entirely concur as with other men who have expressed one. I regret that I am without the influence to serve you at the War Department, but Mr. Lincoln, with whom I have conversed, has, I know, the highest appreciation of your services in this connection. Judge Collamer, whom I regard as among the first of living statesmen and patriots, is enthusiastic in praise of your publications, and, indeed, I have heard but one opinion expressed by all the able men who have referred to them.

Sincerely yours,

R. J. WALKER.†

---

* Richard S. Coxe was a very eminent lawyer from the District of Columbia.

† R. J. Walker was long a Representative in Congress, Secretary of the Treasury under James K. Polk, and was acknowledged as the best financier of his day.

In September of 1861 Miss Carroll prepared a paper on "the Constitutional powers of the President to make arrests and to suspend the writ of *habeas corpus.*" In December, 1861, she published a pamphlet entitled "The War Powers of the Government." This was followed by a paper entitled "The Relation of Revolted Citizens to the National Government." This was written at the especial request of President Lincoln, approved by him, and adopted as the basis of his subsequent action.

WASHINGTON, *January 25, 1861.*

MY DEAR MISS CARROLL :

I read the address of Governor Hicks, which gave me great pleasure. I have been overwhelmed with work and anxiety for North Carolina. I franked all the papers you sent me. It is a great matter for the Union that you hold Maryland firm now.

Go on in your great work. I wish you would say a word for S—— in some of your articles ; he is doing us good, but needs encouragement.

I wish to talk with you on these matters as soon as I can find a moment.

Respectfully and sincerely your friend,

JOHN A. GILMER.*

———

WASHINGTON CITY, *March 11, 1861.*

MY DEAR MISS CARROLL :

I will be pleased to see you to-morrow, any time convenient to yourself, after nine o'clock. I am not seeing

---

* John A. Gilmer was Member of Congress from North Carolina, but a Union man throughout the war.

any one just yet on the matter to which you refer, but, of course, will see *you*. You have my grateful thanks for the great and patriotic services you have rendered and are still rendering to the country in this crisis.

I have the honor to be your friend and servant,

S. P. CHASE.*

WASHINGTON CITY, *April 15, 1862*.

MY DEAR LADY:

I thank you for sending me the last number of your able essays in the New York *Times*. The President paid you a very handsome compliment in the Cabinet meeting yesterday, in reference to your usefulness to the country. He handed your views on colonization and the proper point to initiate the colony, which he said he had requested of you, to Secretary Smith, and said you had given him a better insight into the whole question than any one beside, and you had, on his inquiry, suggested the Interior Department as proper to look after the matter, and advised the Secretary to get into communication with you. This was no more than your desert, but, coming from the President in Cabinet meeting, it was as gratifying to me to hear as it is now to communicate this to you.

With great regard, your obedient servant,

EDWARD BATES.

HOUSE OF REPRESENTATIVES, *May 13, 1862*.

MISS CARROLL:

I send a package by your servant which came here yesterday, I suppose, as I had the honor to frank some of your documents from here. If you will excuse my poor

---

* Salmon P. Chase was U. S. Senator, Governor of Ohio, Secretary of the Treasury, and Chief Judge of the Supreme Court.

writing I will tell you what Mr. Lincoln said about you last night.

I was there with some seven or eight members of Congress and others, when a note and box came from you with products from Central America. He seemed much delighted and read your letter out to us and showed the contents of the box. He said, " This Anna Ella Carroll is the head of the Carroll race. When the history of this war is written she will stand a good bit taller than ever old Charles Carroll did." I thought you might like to hear this.

WM. MITCHELL.

WASHINGTON, D. C., *September 9, 1863.*

MY DEAR MISS CARROLL :

I have read with great pleasure the manuscript left with me. Like all that emanates from your pen, it is profound and able, and I concur with you that its publication would now be timely. As you requested, I forward the package to New York.

Very sincerely and respectfully your friend,

S. P. CHASE.

The Hon. B. F. Wade (then President of the United States Senate) writes from Washington :

March 1, 1869.

MISS CARROLL :

I cannot take leave of public life without expressing my deep sense of your services to the country during the whole period of our national troubles. Although the citizen of a State almost unanimously disloyal and deeply sympathizing with secession, especially the wealthy and aristocratic class of the people, to which you belonged, yet, in the midst of such surroundings, you emancipated your own slaves at a great sacrifice of personal interest, and with your powerful pen defended the cause of the Union and loyalty as ably and effectively as it ever has been defended.

From my position on the Committee on the Conduct of the War I know that some of the most successful expeditions of the war were suggested by you, among which I might instance the expedition up the Tennessee river.

The powerful support you gave Governor Hicks during the darkest hour of your State history prompted him to take and maintain the stand he did, and thereby saved your State from secession and consequent ruin.

All these things, as well as your unremitted labors in the cause of reconstruction, I doubt not are well known and remembered by the members of Congress at that period. I also well know in what high estimation your services were held by President Lincoln, and I cannot leave this subject without sincerely hoping that the Government may yet confer on you some token of acknowledgment for all these services and sacrifices.

Very sincerely, your friend,   B. F. WADE.

BALTIMORE, *September 28, 1869.*

I have known Miss Carroll many years ; she is a daughter of Governor Carroll, and by birth and education entitled to the highest consideration.

She writes exceedingly well, and during the late war published several pamphlets, etc., which I have no doubt proved most serviceable to the cause of the Union. Her own loyalty was ardent and constant through the struggle.

REVERDY JOHNSON.*

---

* Reverdy Johnson—a distinguished lawyer from Maryland, U. S. Senator, Attorney General in Taylor's Cabinet, and Minister to England during Johnson's Administration.

DAYTON, *Nov. 23, 1869.*

MY DEAR MISS CARROLL :

Your letter finds me in the midst of care, labor, and preparation for removal to Washington.

Pardon me, therefore, if I write briefly. You must see
me when the session of Congress commences, that I may
say much for which there is not space or time on paper.
Nobody appreciates more highly than I do your patriotism
and your valuable services with mind and pen through so
many years.

  Yours faithfully and truly,

       ROBERT C. SCHENCK.*

———

LONDON, E. C., *July 30, 1872.*

DEAR MISS CARROLL :

I have read with pleasure the pamphlet you were so kind
as to send me, and am glad to see that your claim is so
strongly endorsed—so strongly that it can hardly be
ignored by Congress.

  Very truly yours,

       H. McCOLLOCH.†

———

WASHINGTON CITY, *January 20, 1873.*

MY DEAR MISS CARROLL :

I owe you an humble apology for not calling to pay my
respects to you, as I intended to do ; but I have been so occupied with numerous engagements that the purpose indicated escaped my recollection until I was on the point of
leaving for my home in Connecticut, and can only now

———

* Robert C. Schenck—General through the war, Member of Congress, and
Minister to England.

† Hugh S. McCulloch was Secretary of the Treasury under Lincoln, Johnson, and Arthur.

proffer to you my cordial and heartfelt wishes for your health, prosperity, and happiness.

I have too much respect for your name and character to address you in the accents of flattery, and I presume you will not suspect me of any such purpose when I say that of the many characters, both male and female, of whom I have formed a favorable opinion since I was introduced into public life, there is no one for whom I cherish a higher esteem than Miss Carroll, of Maryland.

May the richest of Heaven's blessings rest upon your ladyship, and may the inappreciable services which you rendered your country in the dark hour of its peril be recognized by your countrymen, and to a just extent rewarded.

I have the honor to be and to remain, my dear Miss Carroll, most faithfully and truly your friend,

TRUMAN SMITH.*

GREENSBURG, PA., *May 3, 1873.*

MISS CARROLL :

I do remember well that Mr. Lincoln expressed himself in wonder and admiration at your papers on the proper course to be pursued in legislating for the crisis.

In this connection I know that he considered your opinions sound and, coming from a lady, most remarkable for their knowledge of international law.

EDGAR COWAN.†

QUINCY, ILLINOIS, *Sept. 17, 1873.*

MISS A. E. CARROLL :

During the progress of the War of the Rebellion, from 1861 to 1865, I had frequent conversations with President

---

* Truman Smith was a Member of Congress from Connecticut for a long time.

† Edgar Cowan was U. S. Senator from Pennsylvania during the whole war

Lincoln and Secretary Stanton in regard to the active and efficient part you had taken in behalf of the country, in all of which they expressed their admiration of and gratitude for the patriotic and valuable services you had rendered the cause of the Union and the hope that you would be adequately compensated by Congress. At this late day I cannot recall the details of those conversations, but am sure that the salutary influence of your publications upon public opinion and your suggestions in connection with the important military movements were among the meritorious services which they recognized as entitled to remuneration.

In addition to the large debt of gratitude which the country owes you, I am sure you are entitled to generous pecuniary consideration, which I trust will not be withheld.

With sentiments of high regard, I am,

Your obedient servant,

O. H. BROWNING.*

WASHINGTON, D. C., *May 13, 1874.*

MISS A. E. CARROLL:

I am gratified to have the opportunity of expressing my knowledge and appreciation of the valuable services rendered by you to the cause of the Union at the beginning of and during the late war. Being a Marylander and located officially in Baltimore in 1861, 1862, 1863, and 1864, I can speak confidently of the important aid contributed by you to the Government in its struggle with the rebellion. I recollect very distinctly your literary labors, the powerful productions of your pen, which struck terror into the heart of the rebellion in Maryland and encouraged the hopes and stimulated the energies of the loyal sons of our gallant State. Especially do I recall the eminent aid you gave

---

* O. H. Browning, of Illinois, was Senator during the war, in confidential relations with President Lincoln and Secretary Stanton.

to Governor Hicks, and the high esteem he placed upon your services. Indeed, I have reason to know he possessed no more efficent coadjutor, or one whose co-operation and important service he more justly appreciated. I can say with all sincerity I know of no one to whom the State of Maryland—I may say the country at large—is more indebted for singlenesss of purpose, earnestness, and effectivness of effort in behalf of the Government than to yourself.

A failure to recognize these service will indicate a reckless indifference to the cause of true and unfaltering patriotism, to which I cannot think a just Government will prove ungrateful.

I am, dear Miss Carroll, always most sincerely and truly yours,

CHRIS. C. COXE.*

_____

PETERSBORO', N. Y., *May, 1874.*

MISS ANNA ELLA CARROLL :

Surely nothing more can be needed than your pamphlet, entitled " Miss Carroll's Claim before Congress," to insure the prompt and generous payment of it. Our country will be deeply dishonored if you, its wise and faithful and grandly useful servant, shall be left unpaid.

GERRITT SMITH.†

_____

WASHINGTON, D. C., *June 5, 1874.*

DEAR MISS CARROLL :

I did not receive your polite note and the pamphlet in relation to your claim till this morning. The statement of

---

*Cristopher C. Coxe held many offices of trust throughout the war, was quite eminent as a poet and man of letters, and was pension agent at Baltimore.

† Gerritt Smith was a noted philanthropist, Member of Congress, one of the first so-called Abolitionists, and a man of immense wealth.

your case is very strong, both as to the clear proof of "value received" from you by the Government, and on which was founded its promise to pay, and as to the favorable opinions of your literary and military services expressed by leading men. I know of no instance in which a woman not born to sovereign sway has done so much to avert the impending ruin of her country, and that not by cheap valor, like Joan of Arc, but by rare mental ability. As a Marylander, I am proud that the "Old Maryland line" was so worthily represented by you in the struggle for the Union.

You would have had your substantial reward long ago but for the very absurd opinion that by some fixed, mysterious law of nature the labor done by women is worth less than precisely similar work done by men. You should persist in your just claim, if only to establish the principle that the value of work should be estimated according to its merits and not with reference to the worker; but, whatever may be the fate of your demand on the Government, you cannot fail to receive the thanks of the people.

Very respectfully,

SAM'L T. WILLIAMS.

————

PRINCESS ANNE, MD., *August 22, 1874.*

MY DEAR MISS CARROLL :

I have read with interest and gratification the publication respecting your claim now pending before Congress.

I well remember that you were an earnest supporter of the Union in the hour of its trial, and that you did much by word and pen to encourage and sustain those who battled against the rebellion, and for such services you are entitled to high consideration and reward. The proofs adduced are very full and direct. I don't see how its payment can be, resisted without impeaching the evidence of Mr.

Scott, the late Assistant Secretary of War, and of Judge Wade, Chairman of the Committee on the Conduct of War—an alternative which their official and personal characters forbid, even in cases where their personal interests were involved.

With my best wishes, I have the honor to be very truly yours, &c.,

J. W. CRISFIELD.*

CUMBERLAND, MD., *August 25, 1874.*

MY DEAR MISS CARROLL:

You may feel assured that I read with exceeding interest everything from your pen and every reference in the press to yourself and interests. I have no doubt your contribution to the history of Maryland at the eventful crisis referred to will be a most valuable and interesting one.

H. W. HOFFMAN.†

LIMA, PERU, *September 12, 1874.*

MY DEAR MISS CARROLL:

It affords me great pleasure to have an opportunity to testify to the valuable assistance rendered by yourself to the cause of the Union at the commencment and during the progress of the late war. Your private conversations and your publications in the newspapers and pamphlets all tended to inspire that ardent patriotism which a grave crisis in public affairs imperatively demanded. Every Marylander who felt called upon to support the endangered Government of the United States must have been encouraged and cheered in the discharge of a painful duty by that earnest enthusi-

---

* J. W. Crisfield was a Representative from Maryland during the war.
† Henry W. Hoffman was a Representative from Maryland, lawyer, and Member of the House of Representatives.

asm which was at that time displayed by yourself in support of the measures forced upon the Government by the rebellion. I am gratified to hear that you propose to publish a book that will do justice to the memory of the late Governor Hicks ; and offering my best wishes for the success of your undertaking and for your personal health and happiness,

I am sincerely your friend,

FRANCIS THOMAS *

NEWARK, *Sept. 28, 1874.*

DEAR MISS CARROLL :

I have carefully read your pamphlet, and I do not hesitate to say your claim is a strong one. You could not have a better witness than Colonel Scott, a man of the highest character. His testimony is clear and unequivocal, and if your claim is rejected I can attribute it to but one cause— you are a woman—a relic of barbarism against your sex ; but still I believe you will succeed. I am satisfied that a large majority of the members of both Houses are fair-minded, honorable men, disposed to do what is right.

I should be glad to meet you and talk with you about your proposed life of Governor Hicks. There are several matters I should be pleased to discuss with you.

Very truly your friend,

WM H. PARNELL,
President Delaware College.

CHESTERTOWN, MD., *Oct. 9. 1874.*

My friend Miss Carroll has two claims against the Government growing out of services rendered to the country

---

* Francis Thomas was a Member of Congress from Maryland, Governor of Maryland, and Minister to Peru under Grant.

during the civil war—the one of a literary and the other of a military character. Miss Carroll is a daughter of the late Hon. Thomas King Carroll, one of the best men Maryland has ever produced.

GEORGE VICKERS.

———

PRINCETON, *October 13, 1874.*

MISS CARROLL :

I thank you for your letter of the 19th ultimo and for the two pamphlets that accompanied it, which I read with great interest. I think they clearly establish your claim on the gratitude of the country and on a suitable remuneration by Congresss by proving that you rendered the Government very important service during the crisis of the late war. As that service involved great labor and sacrifice on your part and saved the country a great amount of useless expenditure in men and money, justice as well as gratitude demands that it should be liberally rewarded.

Hoping that those in authority will recognize the debt which the country owes you,

I am very respectfully yours,

CHARLES HODGE,
President of Theological Seminary.

———

WASHINGTON, D. C., *December 16, 1874.*

DEAR MISS CARROLL :

I have not the vanity to suppose that my commendation can add to the high estimate placed by all upon your services to the Union in the late war ; but as you have done me the honor to ask a candid expression of my opinion I venture to say that any statesman or author of America might be justly proud of having written such papers as the able pamphlets produced by you in support of the Government at that critical period.

As to your military services in planning the Tennessee campaign, you hold and have published too many proofs of the validity of your claim to require further confirmation.

I shall rejoice in your success in procuring a formal recognition of your labors if only it will aid in establishing the just rule that equal services, whether performed by man or woman, must always command equal recognition and reward.

As a Marylander, I am proud that in the war of the rebellion "the Old Maryland line" was so worthily represented by you.

Samuel T. Williams.

———

The letters of eminent men in admiration of Miss Carroll's papers, published and unpublished, would fill a volume. These are only a portion of those published by order of Congress.

Senator Jacob Howard, of the Military Commission appointed to inquire into Miss Carroll's services, in his report of the 42d Congress, states—

"She did more for the country than all the military generals. She showed where to fight and how to strike the rebellion on the head, possessing withal judicial learning so comprehensive and concise in its style of argument that the Government gladly sat at her feet to learn the wisdom of its powers."

This allusion to military services leads us to a still more remarkable record of Miss Carroll's work.

BENJAMIN F. WADE.

CHAPTER IV.

Early in the fall of 1861 a gunboat fleet was under preparation to descend the Mississippi. It was a time of extreme peril, when the continuance of the Union depended
on immediate military success. The Union armies had
met with repeated reverses. The Confederates were exult-
ant and the European nations were expectant of the approaching downfall of the United States Government.
France had already put forth her hand to control Mexico,
and although in England the Union had warm friends who
still hoped for its success, the general impression was that
its defeat might be considered a foregone conclusion.
Financial ruin also seemed inevitable. The Northern
army was costing the nation two million dollars a day.
The Hon. Mr. Dawes, in a speech in Congress, had declared it "imposssible for the United States to meet this
state of things sixty days longer." "An ignominious
peace," he predicted, "was upon the country and at its
very doors."

At that time there was nothing in the attitude of the Union cause very strongly to appeal to English sympathy. It was openly set forth that the war was not waged for the extermination of slavery. Devotion to the Union could not excite especial interest in any but an American. On the contrary, the prevalent opinion in England was that the United States was a dangerous and rather unscrupulous power, and that it would be for the interests of humanity that it should be divided; consequently the general sympathy was largely with the Confederates and the desires of the governing classes for their success openly avowed. After the emancipation proclamation it was different. The Union cause had thereafter the incalculable advantage of a well-defined moral position—a position always keenly felt by the English masses. The desires of the governing class at that period and the dangers of the position from a military point of view are well indicated in extracts given by Miss Carroll in her successive memorials from the English journals and from diplomatic correspondence.

In an extract from the London *Times*, brought to the notice of the Senate by Mr. Howe, the command of the waters of the southwest is pointed out as the essential matter, and it is stated by Mr· Grimes that " the British Government has sent over into all the British colonies of North America some thirty thousand men."

[London *Times*, September 27 1861.]

" Whatever may be the assertions of the Northerners, they must look upon the permanent separation of the

Southern States and the formation of a second republic as at least highly probable, and in the action of England and France toward Mexico Mr. Lincoln, perhaps, only sees an intervention in the affairs of a country which is soon to be divided from his own by the territory of a rival. * * It is said the three European powers have taken advantage of the dissensions of the American Union to carry out plans upon a violation of the Monroe doctrine."

———

[London *Shipping Gazette*, February 1, 1862.]

" A semi-official note is sent by Napoleon to the British Government respecting the blockade, to the effect that the Emperor cannot longer allow French commerce to be injured."

———

DIPLOMATIC CORRESPONDENCE—CLAY * TO SEWARD.

Jan. 24, 1862.

" Prince Gortchakoff expresses his fears should any reverse happen to us that England would at once make common cause with the South, acknowledge her independence, and finally break down the power of the Republic. I must confess I very much fear England's influence. My first impression is not weakened, but rather strengthened. Nothing but great and decisive success will save us from foreign war. I would prepare for war with England as an essential means to prevent the independence of the South before the first of April."

---

*Cassius **M.** Clay, Minister to St. Petersburg during the Civil War, has been from **first to** last one of Miss Carroll's warm supporters. He says, " Be that **as** it may, your case stands out unique, for you towered above all our generals in military genius, and it would be a shame upon our country if you were not honored with the gratitude of all and solid pecuniary reward." (See p. 132 of batch of memorials.)

Jan. 27, 1862.

* * * " You see our army and our fleet are at Cairo. You see another army and another fleet are behind Columbus, which alone is relied upon to close the Mississippi against us on the north. Though you may not see it, another army and another fleet are actually on their way to New Orleans."

At this time of intense anxiety it was suggested to Miss Carroll by the War Department that she should go West and endeavor to form an opinion as to the probable result of the proposed descent of the Mississippi by the gunboats, upon the success of which the continuance of the Union depended. Accordingly she went to St. Louis, and remaining for a month or more at the Everett House, in that city, by means of maps and charts procured from the Mercantile Library she made careful study of the topography of the proposed line of advance. She became convinced that this intended expedition would result in disaster, and that the Tennessee river, not the Mississippi, would be the true pathway to success.

Again we will turn to Miss Carroll's able account in the Congressional Records of the military position at that time.

" It became evident, in the autumn of 1861, that if the unity of the United States could be maintained by military force, the decisive blow upon the Confederate power must be delivered within sixty or ninety days. To that period the tide of battle had been steadily against the Union, and the military operations had not met the expectations of the country. Nothing is more certain than that this rebel power was able to resist all the power of the Union upon any of the lines of operation known to the Administration ; for operating on any safe base, on any of these known lines, the Union armies were not numerically strong enough to reach the vital point in the Confederate power. The enemy were in strong force on a line extending from the Potomac, westward through Bowling Green, to Columbus, on the Mississippi, and was complete master of all the territory to the Gulf. Kentucky and Missouri had been admitted formally into the Confederacy, and they had resolved to move the Capital to Nashville and extend their battle lines to the northern limits of those States, and the Secretary of War, after a tour of inspection, reported that these States had not sufficient force to hold them to the Union.

The war had then been waged seven months, and between 700,000 and 800,000 men had been mustered in the field ; the public debt aggregated over $500,000,000 ; and the daily average expenses of maintaining the army was upward of $2,000,000, besides the hundreds of precious lives which were being daily sacrificed.

Thus, while the two armies were confronting each other in sight of Washington, events were rapidly pressing in the Southwest which, if unchecked, would change the destiny of the American people for ages to come.

Thus, in that ominous silence which preceded the shock and storm, the two sections stood, each watching and await-

ing the movements of the other. Both were confident;
the South greatly strengthened from her successes and impregnable position ; the North strong in its large excess of
numbers, wealth, and the justice of its cause.

The Army of the Potomac and the Army of the West were
the two expeditions on which the Administration relied.

All others were auxiliary to these great movements. The
first named, though seeming to the country of such signal
moment, occupied a position of comparative insignifi-
cance when contrasted with the army of the Southwest,
and had chance thrown Richmond under national control
at an earlier day it could not have materially affected the
destiny of the war. Capitals in an insurgent and unrecognized power can have but very little strategic value, and
from the geographical position of Richmond it had none
at all, and they were ready to move it any day.

They could have surrendered all the Atlantic States to
Florida and yet maintained their independence ; indeed,
it was upon this theory that the disunion party had ever
based its expectations of separate and independent nation-
ality. Could the Confederates have held their power over
the Mississippi Valley but a few more months they would
have so connected themselves with France through Texas
and with England through the States of the great northwest
as not only to have made good their own independence but
to have dwarfed the United States to the area of their old
thirteen and taken the lead as the controlling political
power on this continent.

With the Mississippi in their possession to the mouth of

the Ohio, the presence of the English and French fleets at New Orleans would have brought about that result.

The Army of the Potomac, after having been put upon a scale of the rarest magnificence consistent with mobility, and with several changes of commanders, took three years and a half to reach Richmond, and was not then half way to a decisive point, and never would have been strong enough had the expedition to open the Mississippi been executed on the plan as originally devised.

Strategically an invasion always leads to deep lines of operations which, on account of the difficulty of maintaining communications with its base, are always dangerous in a hostile country, and every mile the national armies advanced, every victory they gained, carried them farther from their base, and required an increase of force to protect their communications ; while every retreat of the enemy brought him nearer to his resources, and it is mathematically certain that he would soon have reached the point on that line where he would have been the superior power. Nothing but the results of the Tennessee campaign prevented Lee from recruiting his army and extorted from him his sword at Appomatox Court-House.

The Mississippi expedition was designed by the aid of the one from the Gulf to clear the river to the mouth, etc. Could it succeed? Could it open the Mississippi to its mouth? These momentous questions and the military delay were weakening the confidence of the people and confirming foreign powers in the belief that the Government had neither the strength nor the ability to conquer

5 C

the rebellion.   And even could the expedition have opened
the river, was there any point on that river where a decisive
blow could have been dealt the Confederacy?   The Memphis and Charleston railroad, the only complete interior
line of communication, would not necessarily have been
touched.   So long as the Confederacy could maintain its
interior lines of communication complete, the United
States could neither destroy its armies in the east nor open
the Mississippi river.   The National Government could
only escape annihilation by reaching the center of the Confederate power and striking a fatal blow upon its resources.
Geographically, there was but one mode of attack by which
this could be accomplished, and this was unthought of or
unknown to all connected with the prosecution of the war.

Mr. Lincoln saw from the beginning the vital importance of regaining the Mississippi and controlling the resources of its great valley, and therefore reserved to himself
the direction of this expedition as Commander-in-chief.
He was fully alive to the perils that now environed the
Government, and he and his advisers looked imploringly
to the army for relief as the agency absolutely essential
to the nation's life.   This and this only could strike the
blow that must then be struck, if ever.

No display of military genius could have extorted from
Lee his sword so long as his resources were unwasted.   No
valor on the part of our navies and armies could have
opened the Mississippi so long as the Confederates could
keep open the lines of communication.   The Memphis
and Charleston railroad was their only complete bond of

connection between their armies of the east and the armies of the Mississippi Valley. There was but one avenue by which this bond could be reached and effectually severed, and that was the Tennessee river. The people had responded grandly; their uprising in behalf of their endangered Government had astonished the world. It now remained for the army to supplement by its valor in the field what the Administration and the people had done at home.

Never was the stress and strain of a nation more severe; never when another defeat would have been so perilous and a victory so desirable as then. So long as the Confederates were undisturbed in the possession of the southwest, and men and munitions of war sent uninterruptedly to the east, the Army of the Potomac could not advance. Something had to be done to cripple or engage the rebel armies in that section.

As the weary months of October and November wore away, the darkness grew more and more intense and the anxiety more oppressive. A blow had to be inflicted quickly that would be sharp and mortal, to ward off intervention and invasion by European powers, to smother the spirit of secession in southern Illinois and Indiana, and to prevent financial bankruptcy, which of itself must destroy the nation.

And yet neither Mr. Lincoln nor his generals knew or had in mind any plan other than that of forcing a passage down the Mississippi, bristling with batteries that frowned from its bluffs, while swamps and bayous skirted and pierced its banks, affording defenses in the rear little less formidable and forbidding.

And thus the nation stood as in the hush that precedes the storm or the crash of battle, apprehending not so much any particular movement of the Confederate armies as the threatening elements generally with which the air seemed surcharged, and knowing not how or when or where the blow would fall. Military success was of all things most desired ; military delay of all things most dreaded. With the South to stand still was their strength ; time was power, and every day's delay increased the thickening dangers that were closing around the Union cause. With the North not to advance was to recede ; not to dstroy was to be destroyed. The exigencies of the situation made it imperative that the decisive blow should be struck thus early in the war. How to make that advance and deliver that fatal blow was the great problem to be solved. Omniscience only was then able to know whether the last sun had set to rise no more on the Union of these States. The country was clamorous for military successes, but not half so troubled as was Mr. Lincoln and his advisers, for the people did not know, as they did, how much depended thereon ; how the beam trembled in the balance and what irremediable evils were involved in delay.

Congress met ; the Committee on the Conduct of the War was at once created. How great were the dangers which at that supreme moment made the continued existence of the Government a question of doubt, and the fact that the military successes in the West which followed were not achieved a day too soon is made evident by the speeches of many of the most distinguished statesmen of that period, in both houses of Congress, some of them occupying positions on the most important committees connected with the prosecution of the war and necessarily possessed of the most reliable information. The utterances in the halls of Congress sustain every fact as here described."

In this same Congressional document of 1878 Miss Carroll thus describes her inception of the plan of the Tennessee campaign :

"In the autumn of 1861 my attention was arrested by the confidence expressed by Southern sympathizers in the southwest, that the Mississippi could not be opened before the recognition of Southern independence. I determined to inform myself what the pilots thought of the gunboat expedition then preparing to descend the river. On inquiry I was directed to Mrs. Scott, then in the hotel, whose husband was a pilot, and learned from her that he was then with the expedition that had moved against Belmont; and the important facts she gave me increased my wish to see Mr. Scott. On his arrival in St. Louis I sent for him. He said that it was his opinion, and that of all the pilots on these waters, that the Mississippi could not be opened by the gunboats. I inquired as to the navigability of the Cumberland and the Tennessee. He said at favorable stages of water the gunboats could go up the former as high Nashville, and the latter, at all stages, as high as the Muscle Shoals in Alabama. The moment he said the Tennessee was navigable for gunboats the thought flashed upon me that the strongholds of the enemy might be turned at once by diverting the expedition in course of preparation to open the Mississippi up the Tennessee ; and having had frequent conversations with Judge Evans on the military situation, I left the room to communicate this thought—as he had just then called at the hotel—and asked him if it would not have that effect. He concurred that it would, and that it was the move if it was a fact that the Tennessee afforded the navigation ; and he accompanied me to interrogate Mr. Scott, to be satisfied as to the feasibility of the Tennessee. The interview was prolonged some time. At the close I told Mr. Scott it was my purpose to try and induce the Government to divert the Mississippi expedition up the Tennessee, and asked him to give me a memorandum of the most important facts elicited in the conversation, as I wished them for this object. I further stated my intention to pen the history of the war, and requested him to write from time to time all the valu-able information he might be able, and I would remember him in my work. The same day I wrote again to Assistant Secretary of War Thomas A. Scott,* to whom I had prom-ised to communicate the result of my observations while in the West, and also to Attorney General Bates ; to both of whom I urged the importance of a change of campaign."

A letter from Judge Evans, who chanced to be in St. Louis on other business, at the time gives a precisely simi-lar account of this interview with the pilot, and the ideas then suggested by Miss Carroll uttered, as he relates, " in a very earnest and animated manner ! "

Even though it involves some repetition, we will here give

---

*Thomas A. Scott was the great railroad magnate, was Assistant Secre-tary of War when Stanton was Secretary, and was sent by Stanton to inaug-urate the Tennessee campaign which saved the Union.

also an account written by Miss Carroll in the winter of
1889. It will possess an especial interest, as it may be the
last literary exertion that the invalid authoress will ever be
asked to make.

It was called forth by a wish expressed by a leading
magazine to have a fresh account written directly by Miss
Carroll. With fingers lamed by paralysis the following account was written, showing the clearness of Miss Carroll's
memory in her seventy-fifth year.

"In the beginning of the rebellion public opinion gave the
victory to the Southern cause, and no one shared in this
conviction to a greater extent than President Lincoln and
the War Department. The first effort made by me was in
an unpretentious pamphlet, which fell into the hands of Mr.
Lincoln and so pleased him (it did not appear with my
name) that he suggested its adoption as a war measure, and
the satisfaction it gave was so general that Governor Bates,
then Attorney General, urged that I should continue to
write in the interest of the Government. Fired by enthusiasm in a noble cause, I accepted the suggestion, and
followed soon with what some have considered my best
work, "The War Powers of the Government," and other
pamphlets. About this time I had thought of visiting St.
Louis, and mentioned my intention to Col. Thomas A.
Scott, Assistant Secretary of War. He urged me to go,
asking me to write him fully of every point and fact in-
vestigated. These facts I communicated as requested, both
to him and to Governor Bates.

The clouds were dark and lowering. Despair had well

nigh possession of the bravest hearts. After my arrival I soon saw and felt that the sentiment of the West was decidedly against the Union, or rather in favor of the Southern cause.

I visited the various encampments en route and in St. Louis and found but little difference among leading minds as to the result anticipated. All in a measure believed the struggle useless.

Finding the sentiment prevalent that the Union must fall and feeling in my soul that it *must not* fall, I began revolving an escape from the threatened doom. Just then, while I was in St. Louis, the battle of Belmont was fought. When I saw the dead and dying as they lay upon that field and witnessed the sad sight of the ambulance wagons bearing the wounded to the hospitals, my heart sank within me. The future of the war with these awful scenes repeated was a picture not to be endured, and my anxiety as to the result grew still more intense.

In reflecting upon the dangers of the proposed expedition it came upon me, as by inspiration, that the sailors—the pilots—might offer some suggestion. I knew that the military leaders would never avail themselves of this humble source of information. I thought the pilots, of all others, should know the strategic points. Sending for the proprietor of the hotel where I was stopping, I asked him how I could get into contact with any of these men. He told me that the wife of a pilot named Scott was then in the house. I called on her at once and, finding her well informed, I questioned her as to the harbors, coast defenses, etc. Mrs. Scott was just about to leave the city, but she promised to send her husband to me. I could not wait for this chance, but wrote to him for the information I desired. He called upon me in response, and during our conversation he said it would be "death to every man who attempted to go down the Mississippi." Yet no other route had been dreamed of. I then asked him, "What about the Cumberland and Tennessee rivers;" whether they were fordable for gunboats? He replied,"Yes, the Tennessee especially." Of course, he did not at first know of any ulterior purpose in the questions which I was asking, other than the information of an ardent lover of our country. As he mentioned the Tennessee it flashed upon me with the certainty of conviction that I had seen my way to the salvation of my country.

I left the pilot and sent immediately for Judge Evans, of Texas, who was stopping at the same hotel. I was almost overcome with excitement and shall never forget the moment that I rushed to him exclaiming, "What do you think of diverting the army from the Mississippi to the Tennessee!"*

I waited breathlessly for his reply. It came in measured tones. "It may be so. I had never thought of it."

---

*Judge Evans himself, describing this eventful scene, said "that for a moment it seemed as if a halo of glory surrounded Miss Carroll, and that she looked like one transfigured." One hesitates in these matter-of-fact days to repeat such words as these, but as my reliable informant, to whom they were addressed, assures me that such were his words it seemed worth while to record them. In all times it has seemed that the human countenance wholly possessed by a great idea could assume a radiance only to be described by the spectator by some such words as these, and the fact was so symbolized in ancient art. The human soul is no less potent in these days than in the times of old.

That night I wrote to Governor Bates, who had planned the Mississippi gunboat scheme. He presented the letter at once to the Acting Secretary of War, Mr. Scott. They both opposed it at first as impracticable. I returned immediately to Washington, prepared a paper on that basis and took it to Mr. Scott, who was really Acting Secretary of War, General Cameron's time being largely consumed in Cabinet meetings. After reading my plan and hearing my verbal arguments, Mr. Scott's countenance brightened and he exclaimed, " Miss Carroll, I believe you have solved the question." He hurried at once, with the plan in his hands, to the White House and with much excitement gave it to the President. Mr. Lincoln read it with avidity, and when he had finished it Mr. Scott told me that he had never witnessed such delight as he evinced.

General McClellan was then in command. He opposed the plan, but Mr. Lincoln quietly gave the orders himself for a change of base as soon as possible. Up to that time no plan for the close of the struggle, except down the Mississippi, had ever occurred to the mind of any living man or woman, as far as known; but from that moment Mr. Lincoln thought of nothing else. He hastened to send Mr. Scott to investigate, and went himself at once to St. Louis to aid in putting the plan in motion.

Just after the fall of Fort Henry I called at the War Department and saw Mr. Tucker, then Assistant Secretary of War. He told me that Mr. Scott stated to him on leaving for the West, " This is Miss Carroll's plan, and if it succeeds the glory is hers."

General Wade, then chairman of the Committee on the Conduct of the War, was consulted in the matter. He recognized it at once as the right move and openly and boldly approved the plan. Every effort was made to hasten the completion of the gunboats. As soon as they were finished, which was not until February, action was commenced on the Tennessee line. Mr. Wade at the same time made it known to Hon. Wm. Pitt Fessenden, chairman of the Finance Committee in the Senate, that there was then a movement on foot, to be executed as soon as the gunboats, then building at St. Louis, were ready, which would satisfy the entire country and astound the world; and he so reassured the Senate that they calmly waited until the time arrived for the execution of the plan.

Colonel Thomas A. Scott was sent to the West to make all things ready and expedite the movement.

He gave his orders from one point to another, so that when General Halleck, who was then in military command, was notified by Mr. Lincoln that the whole force was to be moved from the Mississippi up the Tennessee river he stood ready for the movement. In February, 1862, the armies moved up the Tennessee, then to Fort Donelson, and then back up the Tennessee to Hamburgh, and two miles from there they fought the battle of Pittsburgh Landing, as pointed out in my plan. Had the movement been strictly carried out from the foot of the Muscle Shoals, in Alabama, Vicksburgh could have been reduced, or Mobile, and the whole thing ended in the spring of 1862 as easily as in 1865, and with the same result. In a recent publication

General Sherman has admitted this fact. At the fall of Fort Henry the country was thoroughly aroused as it never had been before. It was clearly seen that the end was approaching. Richmond was then within reach through Tennessee. For this General McClellan had been waiting. Before this no power on earth could have captured Richmond, and no one knew this better than General McClellan. When the National armies had penetrated into the heart of the South, within two miles of the Memphis and Charleston railroad, the result was plain to every mind.

The old flag displayed in the presence of a million of slaves, who had before been necessarily on the side of their owners, made the fact doubly secure. All hearts were jubilant, and Roscoe Conkling then offered his celebrated resolutions in the House of Representatives to ascertain who it was that had designed these military movements so fruitful in great results; whether they came from Washington or elsewhere; by whom they were designed and what they were intended to accomplish. Judge Olin replied that if it was Mr. Conkling's design to find out who had done this work he could learn by inquiring at the War Department, for certainly the Secretary of War or the President must know all about it; but it was sufficient for the present to know that some one had designed these movements, and that the country was now in the enjoyment of the blessings that had resulted from them. Hon. Thaddeus Stevens moved that the resolutions of Mr. Conkling, making inquiry, be referred to the Military Committee of the House. During the discussion the plan was attributed to one person and another, but no satisfactory proof could be given on any side. I was present through it all and could at any moment have satisfied Congress and the world as to the authorship of the plan, but from prudential reasons I refrained from uttering a word. It was decided to refer the question to the Military Committee of the House, and there the matter slept.''

It is worth while to pause for a moment in our narration to introduce upon the scene one of the most useful and remarkable men of the time, who became one of Miss Carroll's principal coadjutors; this was Senator Wade, of Ohio. He was successively justice of the peace, prosecuting attorney, State senator, judge of the circuit court, and United States Senator for three terms; he was also Acting Vice-President of the United States after Lincoln's death. If President Johnson's impeachment had been carried through he would have been the President for the rest of the term, and it was feared by his opponents that in that case he would have secured the Chicago nomination for the coming term, of which he was one of the candidates.

The first encounter of the Union army, a crowd of raw, undisciplined recruits, under new and inexperienced officers, with the better prepared Confederate army naturally resulted in a tremendous panic. Two carriages were present on the battlefield ; one contained Senators Wade, Chandler, and Brown, Sergeant-at-arms of the Senate, and Major Eaton; in the other was Tom Brown, of Cleveland, Blake, Morris, and Riddle, of the House. Near the extemporized hospital, Ashley's Black Horse sweeping down on the recruits caused

the panic. One of the gentlemen present thus described
the scene. (The description can be met with in Coxe's
Three Decades and in Riddle's Life of Wade, a work that
should be more widely published.)

"It seemed as if the very devils of panic and cowardice
had seized every mortal officer, soldier, teamster, and citizen. No officer tried to rally a soldier or do anything but
spring and run toward Centerville. There was never anything like it for causeless, sheer, absolute, absurd cowardice—
or rather panic—on this miserable earth before. Off they
went, one and all—off down the highway, across the fields,
towards the woods, anywhere, everywhere, to escape. The
further they ran the more frightened they grew, and though
we moved as fast as we could the fugitives passed us by
scores. To enable themselves better to run they threw
away their blankets, knapsacks, canteens, and finally their
muskets, cartridge-boxes—everything. We called to them;
told them there was no danger; implored them to stand.
We called them cowards; denounced them in the most of-
fensive terms; pulled out our heavy revolvers, threatened to
kill them—in vain. A cruel, crazy, hopeless panic possessed them and infected everybody, front and rear."

The two carriages were blocked up in the awful gorge of
Cub's Run and were for a time separated. When they
again met, Mr. Wade shouted, "Boys, we'll *stop* this
damned runaway!"

They found a good position, where a high wall on one
side and a dense impassable wood secured the other side.
The eight gentlemen leaped from their carriages and put

Mr. Wade in command. Mr. Wade, with his hat well back and his famous rifle in his hand, formed them across the pikes all armed with heavy revolvers and facing the onflowing torrent of runaways, who were ghastly sick with panic, and this little band, worthy of the heroes of Thermopylæ, actually kept back the runaway army, so that "for the fourth of an hour not a man passed save McDowell's bearer of dispatches, and he only on production of his papers. The rushing, cowardly, half-armed, demented fugitives stopped, gathered, crowded, flowed back, hedged in by thick-growing cedars that a rabbit could scarcely penetrate. The position became serious. A revolver was discharged, shattering the arm of Major Eaton, from the hand of a mounted escaping teamster" (who had cut loose from his wagon).

"At that critical moment the heroic old Senator and his friends were relieved and probably saved by Colonel Crane and a part of the Second New York, hurrying toward the scene of the disaster, and then the party proceeded. Naturally the exploit of Mr. Wade in stopping a runaway army caused much talk at Washington and increased the great confidence and admiration with which he was already regarded.*

" In consequence of this disaster and the following one at Ball's Bluff, it was evident that both soldiers and officers would have to be created, and that we were without a mili-

---

*A few days ago the present writer was conversing with one of the survivors of the party and received from him a detailed account of this singular episode.

tary commander competent to direct so vast a war. This led to the formation by Congress of a Committee for the Conduct of the War. It consisted of seven members, three from the Senate and four from the House ; Wade, Chandler, and Andrew Johnson from the Senate; Julian, Covode, Gooch, and Odell from the House. (Johnson seems never to have acted.) Nobody but Wade was thought of for chairman. Mr. Wade was absolutely fearless, physically and morally ; absolutely regardless of self ; absolutely devoted to his country. All parties agreed in boundless admiration and confidence in the heroic old Senator. "It is said that Wade seldom missed a session of the committee. The most conscientious of known men; never ill; he never neglected a duty; failed of an engagement ; was never waited for, and never failed to meet his foe, one or many."

"The committee, by Mr. Wade, omitting Mr. Johnson's name, made their first report soon after the close of the 37th Congress, in April, 1863, which made three heavy volumes of over 2,000 printed pages.

Their second report was made May 22, 1865, a trifle more in bulk, six volumes in all." (Very valuable for future historians.)—*Life of Benjamin F. Wade by A. G. Riddle.*

President Lincoln, as Commander-in-Chief, with the assistance of this committee, thereafter directed the movements of the war, all the generals being subordinate and only enlightened step by step as to the accepted plan of campaign, great secrecy being, as Mr. Wade testifies, necessary or the plan would have been frustrated.

CHAPTER V.

MISS CARROLL'S PAPERS TO THE WAR DEPARTMENT—PLAN OF
CAMPAIGN—LETTERS FROM SCOTT, WADE, AND OTHERS—
DISCUSSIONS—PAPERS AS THE CAMPAIGN PROGRESSES.

List of Miss Carroll's papers sent into the War Department
in her own handwriting and signed with her name, originally
on file at the War Department ; all in the first division relating
to the Tennessee campaign ; sent on various occasions to the
Capital to be examined by military committees, and printed by
order of Congress in successive memorials and reports from
1870 to 1881.

The papers marked with a star are now on file at the War
Department. With the permission of the Secretary of War,
these were seen by me and carefully examined March 7th,
1891. They were sent by Robert Lincoln to the Court of Claims
in 1885, and copies were put on file in the office of the Attorney
General, the original documents being returned to the War
Department. One of these original documents at the War Department is now incomplete, but must have been in good order
in 1885, as the copies then made are complete and in excellent
condition. They were verified as true copies by the Secretary
of War. These also were examined by me at the office of the
Attorney General March 23, 1891. The absence of the other
documents from the War Office is accounted for by the remarkable testimony of Benjamin F. Wade and Samuel Hunt (keeper
of the records), as given on page 30, 45th Congress, 2d session,
Mis. Doc. 58, both testifying that the papers were abstracted
from the desk of the Secretary when the Military Committee

6 c   (81)

were considering Miss Carroll's claim, in 1871. As Miss Carroll possessed the original draft of these letters, she quickly reproduced them. The papers having been already examined by the Committee and by Mr. Hunt, the copies were accepted in place of the missing file and printed "by order of Congress," and thus guaranteed they became, to all intents and purposes, the same thing as the original documents; but apparently they were not sent to the War Office, not being the original documents sent from there. On March 20, 1891, I examined the files of the 41st Congress, 2d session, at the Secretary's office of the U. S. Senate, at the Capitol, and there I found Miss Carroll's first memorial, 1870, with the "plan of campaign" attached, just as described by Thomas A. Scott.

S. E. BLACKWELL.

FIRST DIVISION.

A paper usually designated as the "plan of campaign."

When given in at the War Office to Thomas A. Scott it was accompanied by a military map; the paper in Miss Carroll's own handwriting and signed with her name, the map unsigned.

1. November 30, 1862.
2. January 5, 1862.
3. March 26, 1862.
4. May 2, 1862.*
5. May 14, 1862.*
6. May 15, 1862.*
7. Following Monday, 1862.
8. September 9, 1862.*
9. October —, 1862.

The letter to Stanton is on file at the office of the Attorney General, certified as copied from the documents furnished by the War Department in 1885.

(The letter of October, 1862, was also accompanied by a military map, "approved and adopted by the Secretary of War and the President and immediately sent out to the proper military authority." See letter of B. F. Wade, page 24, Mis. Doc. 58, of Memorial, May 18, 1878.)

SECOND DIVISION.

August 25, 1862.
January 31, 1863.
October 7, 1863.
January 11, 1864.
—— —, 1865.

A letter, on file from Robert Lincoln, states that the papers of the second division were returned to Miss Carroll, March 10, 1869.

————

Miss Carroll's first paper, addressed to the War Department, for a campaign on the Tennessee river and thence south, placed in the hands of Hon. Thomas A. Scott, Assistant Secretary of War, the 30th of November, 1861, with accompanying map, is as follows :

" The civil and military authorities seem to be laboring under a great mistake in regard to the true key to the war in the southwest. *It is not the Mississippi, but the Tennessee river.* All the military preparations made in the West indicate that the Mississippi river is the point to which the authorities are directing their attention. On that river many battles must be fought and heavy risks incurred before any impression can be made on the enemy, all of which could be avoided by using the Tennessee river. This river is navigable for middle-class boats to the foot of the Muscle Shoals, in Alabama, and is open to navigation all the year, while the distance is but two hundred and fifty miles, by the river, from Paducah, on the Ohio. The Tennessee offers many advantages over the Mississippi. We should avoid the almost impregnable batteries of the enemy, which cannot be taken without great danger and great risk of life to our forces, from the fact that our boats, if crippled, would fall a prey to the enemy by being swept by the current to him and away from the relief of our friends ; but even should we succeed, still we will only have begun the war, for we shall then fight for the country from whence the enemy derives his supplies.

"Now an advance up the Tennessee river would avoid this danger, for *if our boats were crippled, they would drop back with the current and escape capture ;* but a still greater advantage would be its tendency *to cut the enemy's lines in two by reaching the Memphis and Charleston railroad,* threatening Memphis, which lies one hundred miles due west, and no defensible point between ; also Nashville, only ninety miles northeast, and Florence and Tuscumbia, in North Alabama, forty miles east.

"A movement in this direction would do more to relieve our friends in Kentucky and inspire the loyal hearts in East Tennessee than the possession of the whole of the Mississippi river. If well executed *it would cause the evacuation of all these formidable fortifications* upon which the rebels ground their hopes for success ; and in the event of our fleet attacking Mobile, the presence of our troops in the northern part of Alabama *would be material aid to the fleet.*

"Again, the aid our forces would receive from the loyal men in Tennessee would enable them soon to crush the last traitor in that region, and the separation of the two extremes would do more than one hundred battles for the Union cause.

"The Tennessee river is crossed by the Memphis and Louisville railroad and the Memphis and Nashville railroad. At Hamburg the river makes the big bend on the east, touching the northeast corner of Mississippi, entering the northwest corner of Alabama, forming an arc to the South, entering the State of Tennessee at the northeast corner of Alabama, and if it does not touch the northwest corner of Georgia comes very near it.

"It is but eight miles from Hamburg to the Memphis and Charleston railroad, which goes through Tuscumbia, only two miles from the river, which it crosses at Decatur, thirty miles above, intersecting with the Nashville and Chatta-nooga road at Stevenson. The Tennessee river has never less than three feet to Hamburg on the shoalest bar, and during the fall, winter, and spring months there is always water for the largest boats that are used on the Mississippi river.

"It follows, from the above facts, that in making the Mis-sissippi the key to the war in the West, or rather in over-looking the Tennessee river, the subject is not understood by the superiors in command."

Extracts from a second paper, January 5, 1862, giving additional particulars for the advance up the Tennessee:

"Having given you my views of the Tennessee river on my return from the West, showing that this river is the true strategical key to overcome the rebels in the southwest, I beg again to recur to the importance of its adoption. This river is never impeded by ice in the coldest winter, as the Mississippi and the Cumberland sometimes are. I ascertained, when in St. Louis, that the gunboats then fitting out could not retreat against the current of the western rivers, and so stated to you; besides, their principal guns are placed forward and will not be very efficient against an enemy below them. The fighting would have to be done by their stern guns—only two ; or if they anchored by the stern they would lose the advantage of motion, which would prevent the enemy from getting their range. Our gunboats at anchor would be a target which the enemy will not be slow to improve and benefit thereby.

"The Tennessee river, beginning at Paducah fifty miles above Cairo, after leaving the Ohio, runs across south-south-east, rather than through Kentucky and Tennessee, until it reaches the Mississippi line directly west of Florence and Tuscumbia, which lie fifty miles east, and Memphis, one hundred and twenty-five miles west, with the Charleston and Memphis railroad eight miles from the river. There is no difficulty in reaching this point at any time of the year, and the water is known to be deeper than on the Ohio.

"If you will look on the map of the Western States you will see in what a position Buckner would be placed by a strong advance up the Tennessee river. He would be obliged to back out of Kentucky, or, if he did not, our forces could take Nashville in his rear and compel him to lay down his arms."

Testimony of Thomas A. Scott, Assistant Secretary of War, to Hon. Jacob M. Howard, chairman of the Military Committee, to consider the claim presented by Miss Carroll in 1870:

PHILADELPHIA, *June 24, 1870.*

On or about the 30th of November, 1861, Miss Carroll, as stated in her memorial, called on me, as the Assistant Secretary of War, and suggested the propriety of abandoning the expedition which was then preparing to descend the Mississippi, and to adopt instead the Tennessee river, and handed to me the plan of campaign, as appended to her memorial; which plan I submitted to the Secretary of War, and its general ideas were adopted. On my return from the southwest in 1862 I informed Miss Carroll, as she states in her memorial, that through the adoption of this plan the county had been saved millions, and that it entitled her to the kind consideration of Congress.

THOMAS A. SCOTT.

To the Military Committee, appointed for that purpose in 1872:

Hon. JACOB M. HOWARD, of the Military Committee or the United States Senate.

Again:

PHILADELPHIA, *May 1, 1872.*

MY DEAR SIR:

I take pleasure in stating that the plan presented by Miss Carroll in November, 1861, for a campaign upon the Tennessee river and thence south, was submitted to the Secretary of War and President Lincoln, and after Secretary Stanton's appointment I was directed to go to the Western armies and arrange to increase their effective force as rapidly as possible. A part of the duty assigned me was the organization and consolidation into regiments of all the troops then being recruited in Ohio, Indiana, Illinois, and Michigan, for the purpose of carrying through this campaign, then inaugurated. This work was vigorously prosecuted by the army, and as the valuable suggestions of Miss Carroll, made to the Department some months before, were substantially carried out through the campaigns in that section, great success followed, and the country was largely benefited in the saving of time and expenditure.

I hope Congress will reward Miss Carroll liberally for her patriotic efforts and services.

Very truly yours,

THOMAS A. SCOTT.

————

Letter from the Hon. Benjamin F. Wade, appended to the report of General Bragg, of the Military Committee, of March 3, 1881 :

DEAR MISS CARROLL ·

I had no part in getting up the Committee [on the Conduct of the War]. The first intimation to me was that I had been made the head of it ; but I never shirked a public duty, and at once went to work to do all that was possible to save the country. We went fully into the examination of the several plans for military operations then known to the Government, and we saw plainly enough that the time it must take to execute any of them would make it fatal to the Union.

We were in the deepest despair, until just at this time Colonel Scott informed me that there was a plan already devised which, if executed with secrecy, would open the Tennessee and save the national cause. I went immediately to Mr. Lincoln and talked the whole matter over.

He said he did not himself doubt that the plan was feasible, but said there was one difficulty in the way ; that no military or naval man had any idea of such a movement, it being the work of a civilian, and none of them would believe it safe to make such an advance upon only a navigable river, with no protection but a gunboat fleet, and they would not want to take the risk. He said it was devised by Miss Carroll, and military men were extremely jealous of all outside interference. I pleaded earnestly with him, for I found there were influences in his Cabinet then averse to his taking the responsibility, and wanting everything done in deference to the views of McClellan and Halleck. I said to Mr. Lincoln : " You know we are now in the last extremity, and you have to choose between adopting and at once executing a plan which you believe to be the right one and save the country, or defer to the opinions of military men in command and lose the country." He finally decided he would take the initiative ; but there was Mr. Bates, who had suggested the gunboat fleet, and wanted to advance down the Mississippi, as originally designed ; but after a little he came to see that no result could be achieved on that mode of attack, and he united with us in favor of the change of expedition as you recommended.

After repeated talks with Mr. Stanton I was entirely convinced that, if placed at the head of the War Department, he would have your plan executed vigorously, as he fully believed it was the only means of safety, as I did. Mr. Lincoln, on my suggesting Stanton, asked me how the leading Republicans would take it ; that Stanton was fresh from the Buchanan Cabinet, and many things were said of him.*
I insisted he was our man withal, and brought him and Lincoln into communication, and Lincoln was entirely

---

* Stanton had been the bitterest of Democrats. The Republicans then knew nothing certainly of his course in Buchanan's Cabinet. His appointment surprised the Senate. Wade knew and endorsed him there. That was sufficient.—*Riddle's Life of Wade.*

satisfied.   But so soon as it got out, the doubters came to
the front.   Senators and members called on me.   I sent
them to Stanton and told them to decide for themselves.
The gunboats were then nearly ready for the Mississippi
expedition, and Mr. Lincoln agreed, as soon as they were,
to start the Tennessee movement.   It was determined that
as soon as Mr. Stanton came into the Department, then
Colonel Scott should go out to the Western armies and
make ready for the campaign in pursuance of your plan, as
he has testified before committees.   It was a great work to
get the matter started ; you have no idea of it.   We almost
fought for it.   If ever there was a righteous claim on earth,
you have one.   I have often been sorry that, knowing all
this as I did then, I had not publicly declared you as the
author ; but we were fully alive to the importance of absolute secrecy.   I trusted but few of our people ; but to pacify
the country I announced from the Senate that the armies
were about to move, and inaction was no longer to be toler-
ated.   Mr. Fessenden, head of the Finance Committee, who
had been told of the proposed advance, also stated in the
Senate that what would be achieved in a few more days
would satisfy the country and astound the world.

As the expedition advanced, Mr. Lincoln, Mr. Stanton,
and myself frequently alluded to your extraordinary sagacity
and unselfish patriotism, but all agreed that you should be
recognized for your most noble service and properly rewarded for the same.

The last time I saw Mr. Stanton he was on his death-
bed ; he was then most earnest in his desire to have you
come before Congress, as I told you soon after, and said
that if he lived he would see that justice was awarded you.
This I have told you often since, and I believe the truth in
this matter will finally prevail.

B. F. WADE.

JEFFERSON, OHIO, *July 27, 1876.*

MY DEAR MISS CARROLL:

Yours of the 22nd is at hand and its contents noticed, but I cannot perceive, myself, that it is necessary for you to procure any further testimony to prove to all unprejudiced minds that you were the first to discover the importance of the Tennessee river in a military point of view, and was the first to discover that said river was navigable for heavy gunboats; and to ascertain these important facts you made a journey to that region, and with great labor and expense, by examination of pilots and others, and that with these facts you drew up a plan of campaign which you, I think, first exhibited to Colonel Scott, who was then Assistant Secretary of War, which was shown to the President and Mr. Stanton, which information and plan caused the immediate change of the campaign from the Mississippi to the Tennessee river, and this change, with all the immense advantages to the national cause, was solely due to your labor and sagacity. I do not regard it as an impeachment of the military sagacity of the officers on either side that they had not seen all this before, but I suppose none of them knew or believed the Tennessee river to be navigable for such craft, for had the Confederate officers known all this it would have been easy for them to have so fortified its banks as to have made such an expedition impossible.

Now all the above facts are proved beyond doubt, unless the witnesses are impeached; but all should bear in mind that when the Government had concluded to make this important change from the Mississippi to the Tennessee the utmost secrecy was absolutely necessary or the whole plan might have been frustrated by the enemy, and it was so kept that even members of Congress and Senators never could ascertain who was entitled to the honor of the plan, as can be seen by their endeavors to find out by consulting

the *Congressional Globe*, etc. * * * Where is Judge
Evans and how is his health? I am anxious to hear from
him, whom I regard as one of the best of men. Give him
my best respects.

Truly yours,

B. F. WADE.

———

WESTMINSTER PALACE HOTEL,
LONDON, *November 29, 1875.*

MY DEAR MISS CARROLL :

I remember very well that you were the first to advise the
campaign on the Tennessee river in November, 1861.
This I have never heard doubted, and the great events
which followed it demonstrated the value of your suggestions. This will be recognized by our Government, sooner
or later, I cannnot doubt. On reaching home I hope to
shake you by the hand once more.

Sincerely your friend,

REVERDY JOHNSON.

———

*Discussions in Congress Showing the Critical Nature of the
Situation.*

IN THE HOUSE, *January 7, 1862.*

Mr. KELLEY : I think the condition of this Capital to-day
invites war. It is environed within a narrow circle of two
hundred thousand men in arms, and yet, sir, that short river
which leads to the Capital of a great and proud country, thus
defended and encircled by patriot troops, is so thoroughly
blockaded by rebels that the Government, though its army
has not an adequate supply of forage, cannot bring upon it
a peck of oats to feed a hungry horse. * * * Call it what

you may, it is a sight at which men may well wonder. We have six hundred thousand men in the field. We have spent I know not how many millions of dollars, and what have we done? What one evidence of determined war or military skill have we exhibited to foreign nations, or to our own people? * * * We have been engaged in war for seven months. * * * England does respect power. * * * Let her hear the shouts of a victorious army, and England and the powers of the continent will pause with bated breath. Sir, it was said yesterday the last days had come. My heart has felt the last day of our dear country was rapidly approaching. Before we have reached victory we have reached bankruptcy. We are to-day flooding the country with an irredeemable currency. In ninety days, with the patriotism of the people paralyzed by the inaction of our great army, the funded debt of the country will depreciate with a rapidity that will startle us. In ninety days more the nations of the world will, I fear, be justified in saying to us, "You have no more right to shut up the cotton fields of the world by a vain and fruitless effort to reconquer the territory now in rebellion than China or Japan has to wall themselves in, and in the eyes of international law, in the eyes of the world, and, I fear, in the eyes of impartial history, they will be justified in breaking our blockade and giving to the rebels means and munitions of war. * * * But, sir, in less than ninety days, to come back to the point of time, we shall be advancing in the month of April, when Northern men will begin to feel the effects of heat in the neighborhood of Ship Island and the mouth of the Mississippi. Looking at the period of ninety days, I say it is not a double but a triple edged sword approaching, perhaps, the single thread of destiny upon which the welfare of our country hangs. Bankruptcy and miasmatic pestilence are sure to come within the lapse of that period, and foreign war may add its horror to theirs.

Mr. WRIGHT : We are gasping for life. This great Government is upon the brink of a volcano, which is heaving to and fro, and we are not certain whether we exist or no.

Mr. F. A. CONKLING : In this crisis of our history, when the very existence of the Republic is threatened, when in all human probability the next thirty days will decide forever whether the Union is to maintain its place among the powers of the earth or whether it is to go down and constitutional liberty is to perish. * * *

IN THE HOUSE, *January 20, 1862.*

Mr. WRIGHT: There is one great abiding and powerful issue to-day, and that is the issue whether the country and the Constitution shall be saved or whether it shall be utterly and entirely annihilated. With Pennsylvania it is a question of national existence, of life or death. * * * The great heart of Pennsylvania is beating to-day for the cause of the Union. * * * It is to decide the great question whether the liberty which has been handed down to us by our fathers shall be permitted to remain in the land, or whether chaos or desolation shall blot out the country and Government forever.

In the Senate, *January 22, 1862.*

Mr. WADE: But, sir, though the war lies dormant, still there is war, and it is not intended that it shall stay in this quiescent state much longer. The committee to which I belong are determined * * * that it shall move with energy. If the Congress will not give us, or give themselves, power to act with efficiency in war, we must confide everything to the Executive Government and let them usurp everything. If you would not fix your machinery so that you might advise with me and act with me, * * * I would act independent of you, and you might call it what you please. This is for the suppression of the rebellion, and the measures that we are to sit in secrecy upon look to that end and none other. No measure rises in importance above that connected with the suppression of the rebellion. * * * We stand here for the people and we act for them. * * * There is no danger to be apprehended from any secrecy which, in the consideration of war measures, we may deem it proper to adopt. It is proper for us, as it is for the general in the field, as it is for your Cabinet ministers, to discuss matters in secret when they pertain to war.

In the House, *January 22, 1862.*

Mr. THADDEUS STEVENS: * * * Remember that every day's delay costs the nation $1,500,000 and hundreds of lives. * * * What an awful responsibility rests upon those in authority; their mistakes may bring mourning to the land and sorrow to many a fireside. * * * If we cannot save our honor, save at least the lives and the treasure of the nation.

About this time Miss Carroll was spoken of by those conversant with her plans as "the great unrecognized member of Lincoln's Cabinet." But, glorious as was the success, Miss Carroll's plans were not fully carried out, to the great after regret of the War Department, who recognized that the war, which might then have been brought to a speedy termination, had been greatly prolonged through the omission.

Miss Carroll continued her communications to the War Department, endeavoring to rectify mistakes.

Extract from Miss Carroll's letter to the Department on the reduction of Island No. 10, and pointing out the advantages of the immediate seizure of the Memphis and Charleston railroad, March 26, 1862.

"The failure to take Island No. 10, which thus far occasions much disappointment to the country, excites no surprise in me. When I looked at the gunboats at St. Louis and was informed as to their power, and considered that the current of the Mississippi at full tide runs at the rate of five miles per hour, which is very near the speed of our gunboats, I could not resist the conclusion that they were not well fitted to the taking of batteries on the Mississippi river if assisted by gunboats perhaps equal to our own. Hence it was that I wrote Colonel Scott from there that the Tennessee was our strategic point, and the successes at Fort Henry and Donelson established the justice of these observations. Had our victorious army, after the fall of Fort Henry, immediately pushed up the Tennessee river and taken a position on the Memphis and Charleston railroad, between Corinth, Mississippi, and Decatur, Alabama, which might easily have been done at that time with a small force, every rebel soldier in Western Kentucky and Tennessee would have fled from every position to the south of that railroad ; and had Buell pursued the enemy in his retreat from Nashville, without delay, into a commanding position in North Alabama, on the railroad between Chattanooga and Decatur, the rebel government at Richmond would have necessarily been obliged to retreat to the cotton States. I am fully satisfied that the true policy of General H—— is to strengthen Grant's column by such force as will enable him at once to seize the Memphis and Charleston railroad, as it is the readiest means of reducing Island 10 and all the strongholds of the enemy to Memphis.''

Letter written from St. Louis, military headquarters for the Southwest :

* St. Louis, *May 2, 1862.*

'' I think the war on the approaches to the Tennessee river has ended. I think the enemy will retreat to the Grand Junction, some sixty miles nearer Memphis ; and when our forces approach him there, he will go down the Central Mississippi railroad to Jackson, and if there is another great battle in the West it will be there. I think they will try to postpone anything serious until after the pending battles in Virginia. If they make the attempt now every leader would be taken in the event of defeat, without

---

* Copied by me on March 23, 1891, from the file at the office of the Attorney General.   S. E. BLACKWELL.

7 C

fail, whilst if it is postponed until after the fate of Virginia is decided the leaders can bring what troops they have left and, joining them to what they have here, make one last struggle for life, and if defeated they can escape across the Mississippi into Arkansas, and through that into Texas and Mexico. You may rest assured the *leaders* will not be caught if they can get away with life ; and as to *property*, they have *that* secured already. The only way this plan can be frustrated is to occupy Memphis and Vicksburg strongly, *particularly* the *latter*, and send one or more of our gunboats up the *Yazoo* river *to watch every creek and inlet*, so that they may be unable to get across the *swamps* by *canoes* and *skiffs*.

" I have heard that all the skiffs and canoes have been taken from Memphis and Vicksburg to some point up the *Yazoo river* and fitted up, for what purpose I do not know, but I can think there is no other than what I name, for *one night's ride* from Jackson will carry a man to the edge of the *Yazoo* river *swamps*, where it would be impossible to follow unless equally well acquainted and with boats like theirs. From there their escape would be easy, as *they would have 400 miles* of the river to strike, at any part of which they would find friends to assist them over to the Arkansas side of the river, and from *there* pursuit would be useless."

* Letter from Miss Carroll to Secretary Stanton :

May 14, 1862.

Hon. E. M. STANTON, *Secretary of War :*

It will be the obvious policy of the rebels, in the event

---

* Written to recommend Pilot Scott for information given.

of Beauregard's defeat, to send a large column into Texas
for the purpose of holding that country for subsistence,
where beef and wheat abound. Now, all this can be defeated by strongly occupying Vicksburg and plying a gunboat or two on the Yazoo river. I would also suggest a
gunboat to be placed at the mouth of the Red and Arkansas rivers. Whether the impending battle in North Mississippi should occur at Corinth or within the area of a hundred miles, a large part of the enemy's forces will retreat
by the Yazoo river and by the railroad to Vicksburg, on the
Mississippi, and will then take the railroad through Louisiana into Texas. I handed Honorable Mr. Watson on
Monday a letter giving information that the canoes, skiffs,
and other transports had been sent up the Yazoo river from
Memphis and Vicksburg for the ·purpose, undoubtedly, of
securing the rebels' retreat from our pursuing army.

This information I obtained from Mr. Scott, a pilot on
the *Memphis,* which conducted the retreat of the soldiers
at the battle of Belmont, and had been with the fleet in the
same capacity up the Tennessee river. Until June last he
resided in New Orleans, and for twenty years or more has
been in his present employment. His ·wife stated this to
me, and with a view of obtaining facts about that section
of country I requested her to introduce him to me. I was
surprised at his general intelligence in regard to the war,
and from the facts I derived from him and other practical
men I satisfied myself that the Tennessee river was the true
strategic point, and submitted a document to this effect to
Hon. Thomas A. Scott, dated the 30th of November, 1861,
which changed the whole programme of the war in the
Southwest, and inured to the glory of our arms in that section and throughout the land. The Government is not
aware of the incalculable service rendered by the facts I
learned from this pilot, and I therefore take the present
occasion to ask his promotion to the surveyorship of New

Orleans, for which I should think him well suited in this crisis.

I enclose you a letter describing the battle of Pittsburg Landing, which will interest you.

Very sincerely,

ANNA ELLA CARROLL.

Extract from the letter to the Secretary of War on the 15th of May, 1862, advising the occupation of Vicksburg :

* * * " It will be the obvious policy of the rebels, in the event of Beauregard's defeat, to send a large column into Texas for the purpose of holding that country for subsistence, where beef and wheat abound. This can be defeated by strongly occupying Vicksburg and plying a gunboat, to be placed at the mouth of the Red and Arkansas rivers." * * * " Whether the impending battle in North Mississippi should occur at Corinth or within the area of a hundred miles, a large part of the enemy's forces will retreat by the Yazoo river, and by the railroad to Vicksburg, on the Mississippi, and will take the railroad through Louisiana into Texas." * * *

On the following Monday Miss Carroll handed Mr. Watson a letter giving information that the canoes, skiffs, and other transports had been sent up the Yazoo from Memphis and Vicksburg for the purpose, undoubtedly, of securing the rebels' retreat from our pursuing army.

Letter from the file of the Attorney General, Court of Claims : *

Hon. E. M. STANTON, *Secretary of War :*

SIR : I find that the Secretary of War and the President are violently assailed for arresting certain parties in the loyal States and suspending the writ of *habeas corpus.* It is represented that a high judicial officer in the State of Vermont has taken issue with the Administration on this question. It is also intimated that the State authorities, in Vermont and elsewhere, are to be invoked for the protection of the citizen against military arrests. There is very great danger at this time to be apprehended to the country from a conflict between the military and the judicial authorities, because the opinion is almost universal that the authority to suspend the writ of *habeas corpus* rests with Congress. The reason that this opinion has so generally obtained is that in England, whence we have derived much of our political and judicial system, the power to suspend the writ is vested alone in Parliament ; and our jurists, without reflecting upon the distinction between the constitutions of the two Governments, have erroneously made the English theory applicable to our own.

I believe in my work on the "War Powers of the Government," etc., I was the first writer who has succeeded in placing the power of the Government to arrest for political offences, and to suspend the writ of *habeas corpus,* on its true foundation. In the opinion of eminent men, if this work were now placed in the hands of every lawyer and judge it would stay the evil which threatens to arise from a conflict between the military and judicial departments of the country. I therefore respectfully suggest the propriety of authorizing me to circulate a large edition of

---

* Copied by me from the file at the office of the Attorney General, March 23, 1891. S. E. BLACKWELL.

this work, or, what would be still better, that I should write a *new paper*, specially on the power of the Executive to suspend the writ of *habeas corpus*, and to arrest political offenders.

ANNA ELLA CARROLL.

In October, 1862, Miss Carroll wrote the following letter to the Secretary of War, through the hands of John Tucker, Assistant Secretary, on the reduction of Vicksburg :

" As I understand an expedition is about to go down the river for the purpose of reducing Vicksburg, I have prepared the enclosed map in order to demonstrate more clearly the obstacles to be encountered in the contemplated assault. In the first place, it is impossible to take Vicksburg in front without too great a loss of life and material, for the reason that the river is only about half a mile wide, and our forces would be in point-blank range of their guns, not only from their water batteries, which line the shore, but from the batteries that crown the hills, while the enemy would be protected by the elevation from the range of our fire. By examining the map I enclose you will at once perceive why a place of so little apparent strength has been enabled to resist the combined fleets of the upper and lower Mississippi. The most economical plan for the reduction of Vicksburg now is to push a column from Memphis to Corinth, down the Mississippi Central railroad to Jackson, the capital of the State of Mississippi. *The occupation of Jackson and the command of the railroad to New Orleans would compel the immediate evacuation of Vicksburg*, as well

as the retreat of the entire rebel army east of that line, and
by another movement of our army from Jackson, Mississippi,
or from Corinth to Meridian, in the State of Mississippi, on
the Ohio and Mobile railroad, especially if aided by a
movement of our gunboats on Mobile, the Confederate
forces, with all the disloyal men and their slaves, would be
compelled to fly east of the Tombigbee. Mobile being then
in our possession, with 100,000 men at Meridian we would
redeem the entire country from Memphis to the Tombigbee
river. Of course I would have the gunboats with a small
force at Vicksburg as auxiliary to this movement. With regard to the canal, Vicksburg can be rendered useless to the
Confederate army upon the first rise of the river; but I do
not advise this, because Vicksburg belongs to the United
States and we desire to hold and fortify it, for the Mississippi river at Vicksburg and the Vicksburg-Jackson railroad
will become necessary as a base of our future operations.
Vicksburg might have been reduced eight months ago, as I
then advised, after the fall of Fort Henry, and with much
more ease than it can be done to-day."

WASHINGTON, D. C., *May 10, 1876.*

MY DEAR MISS CARROLL:

Referring to the conversation with Judge Evans last evening, he called my attention to Colonel Scott's telegram,
announcing the fall of Island No. 10, in 1862, as endorsing
your plan, when Scott said: "The movement in the rear
has done the work." I stated to the Judge, as he and you
knew before, that your paper on the reduction of Vicksburg

did the work on that place, after being so long baffled and with the loss of so much life and treasure, by trying to take it from the water ; that to my knowledge your paper was approved and adopted by the Secretary of War and the President, and immediately sent out to the proper military authority in that Department.

I remember well their remarks upon it at that time, and of all your other views and suggestions, made after we got the expedition inaugurated, and know the direction they took. These matters were often talked over as the campaign advanced, and in the very last interview with Mr. Stanton, just before his death, he referred to your services in originating the campaign in the strongest terms he could express, and, as I have informed you, stated that if his life was spared he would discharge the great duty of seeing your services to the country properly recognized and rewarded. But why need I say more. Your claim is established beyond controversy, unless the witnesses are impeached, and I hardly think they would undertake that business. What motive could any of us have had to mislead or falsify the history of the war. Your claim is righteous and just, if ever there was one, and for the honor of my country I trust and hope you will be suitably rewarded and so declared before the world.

Yours truly,

B. F. WADE.

———

Miss Carroll's after papers, so far as I can learn, were mainly on emancipation, on the ballot, and on reconstruction.

CHAPTER VI.

Very curious is the picture revealed by the Congressional records. Fully as Lincoln and his Military Committee recognize the genius of the remarkable woman now taking the lead, it needs great courage to adopt her plans.

" Mr. Lincoln and Stanton are opposed to having it known that the armies are moving under the plan of a civilian, directed by the President as Commander-in-Chief. Mr. Lincoln says it was that which made him hesitate to inaugurate the movement against the opinions of the military commanders, and he says he does not want to risk the effect it might have upon the armies if they found that some outside party had originated the campaign ; that he wanted the country and the armies to believe they were doing the whole business in saving the country."

Judge Wade alludes to a remark about the sword of Gideon, made by Secretary Stanton, and says that was done to maintain the policy of secrecy as to the origin of the plan. Strict silence is counselled as absolutely neccessary, and Anna Ella Carroll is not the woman to allow a thought of self to interfere with her plans for the salvation of her country.

(105)

Rapid and brilliant is the success of that Tennessee campaign, planned and supervised by that able head. Her papers, as the campaign progresses, are as remarkable as the original plan. On the fall of Fort Henry she prepares a paper on the feasibility of advancing immediately on Mobile or Vicksburg, without turning to the right or left. She carries it, in person, to the War Department and delivers it into the hands of Assistant Secretary Tucker, who takes it at once to the Secretary of War.

She exhibits also a copy of the original plan, submitted on the 30th of November, 1861.

Mr. Tucker remarks: "This is prophecy fulfilled so far," and says he knows her to be the author, Colonel Scott having so informed him before he left for the West.

Notwithstanding some blunders in the execution, the campaign progresses, as the authorities at the War Office testify, "mainly in accordance with Miss Carroll's suggestions."

The fall of Fort Henry having opened the navigation of the Tennessee river, its capture is followed by the evacuation of Columbus and Bowling Green. Fort Donelson is given up and its garrison of 14,000 troops are marched out as prisoners of war; Pittsburg Landing and Corinth follow. The Confederate leaders discover with consternation that the key to the whole situation has been found. All Europe rings with the news of victories that have reversed the probabilities of the war.

On the 10th of April, four months after the adoption of Miss Carroll's plans, President Lincoln issues a proclamation thanking Almighty God for the "signal victories which have saved the country from foreign intervention and invasion."

THE FOREIGN MINISTERS ARE ENRAPTURED.

SEWARD TO DAYTON.

March 6, 1862.

"It is now apparent that we are at the beginning of the end of the attempted revolution. Cities, districts, and States are coming back under Federal authority."

ADAMS TO SEWARD.

March 6, 1862.

"We are anxiously awaiting the news by every steamer, but not for the same reasons as before; the pressure for interference here has disappeared."

DAYTON TO SEWARD.

March 25, 1862.

"The Emperor said that he must frankly say that when the insurrection broke out and this concession of belligerent rights was made he did not suppose the North would succeed; that it was the general belief of the statesmen of Europe that the two sections would never come together again."

DAYTON TO SEWARD.

March 31, 1862.

"I again called the Emperor's attention to the propriety of his Government retracing its steps in regard to its concession to the insurrectionists of belligerent rights, referring him to the consideration in regard thereto contained in your former dispatches. He said, 'It would scarcely be worthy of a great power, now that the South was beaten, to withdraw a concession made to them in the day of their strength.'"

PRESIDENT LINCOLN'S PROCLAMATION.

April 10, 1862.

"It has pleased Almighty God to vouchsafe signal victories to the land and naval forces engaged in suppressing an internal rebellion, and at the same time to avert from our country the danger of foreign intervention and invasion."

SEWARD TO DAYTON.

May 7, 1862.

"The proclamation of commerce which is made may be regarded by the maritime powers as an announcement that the Republic has passed the danger of disunion."

Great enthusiasm is felt at Washington and throughout the country, as it becomes evident that a brilliant and successful plan has been adopted, and great anxiety is evinced to find out and reward the author.

For this purpose a lively debate takes place in the House of Representatives for the avowed purpose of finding out whether "these victories were arranged or won by men sitting at a distance, engaged in organizing victory," or whether "they have been achieved by bold and resolute men left free to act and to conquer." No one knows.

Mr. Conkling proposes to "thank Halleck and Grant."

Mr. Washburne thinks "General McClernand and General Logan should be included."

Mr. Cox thinks "General Smith is entitled to an equal degree of the glory."

Mr. Holman thinks "General Wallace should have a fair share."

Mr. Mallory thinks "General Buell should not be forgotten."

Mr. Kellogg thinks all these suggestions derogatory to President Lincoln, as Commander-in-Chief. He desires "it to be remembered that subordinate officers by law are under the control and command of the Commander-in-Chief of the American Army." He believes "there is, emanating from the Commander-in-Chief of the American forces, through his first subordinates, and by them to the next, and so continuously down to the soldiers who fight upon the battlefield, a well digested, clear, and definite policy of campaign, that is in motion to put down this rebellion ; " and he "here declares that he believes that the system of movements that has culminated in glorious victories, and which will soon put down this rebellion, finds root, brain, and execution in the Commanding General of the American Army and the Chief Executive of the American people."

Mr. Olin says : " If it be the object of the House, before passing a vote of thanks, to ascertain who was the person who planned and organized these victories, then it would be eminently proper to request the Secretary of War to give us that information. That would satisfy the gentleman and the House directly as to who was the party that planned these military movements. It is sufficient for the present that somebody has planned and executed these military movements. Still, if the gentleman has any desire to know who originated these movements, he can ascertain that fact by inquiring at the proper office, for certainly some one at the War Department must be informed on the subject. The Secretary of War knows whether he had anything to do with them or not ; the Commanding General knows whether he had anything to do with them or not. If neither of them had anything to do with them, they will cheerfully say so."

But at the War Department it has been determined that the secret must be kept so long as the war continues, and this noble, silent woman sits in the gallery listening to all this discussion and makes no claim, knowing well the injury that it would be to the national cause if it should be known that the plan was the work of a civilian, and, above all, a *woman*—a creature despised and ignored, not even counted as one of " the people " in the sounding profession made of human rights a hundred years ago.

The House of Representatives having failed to discover the author of the campaign, on March 13th, 1862, the Senate makes a similar attempt.

Mr. Washburne and Mr. Grimes think "it is Commodore Foote who should be thanked." But no one knows.

Again that wonderful, quiet woman in the gallery sits silently listening to all their talking and discussing.

She speaks of it afterwards to Colonel Scott ; refers to the discussions which had taken place in Congress to find out who had devised the movement, and to the fact that she had preserved entire silence while the debate went on, claiming it for one and another of the generals of the war.

Colonel Scott says she has " acted very properly in the matter ; that there is no question of her being entitled to the vote of thanks by Congress ; that she has saved incalculable millions to the country, etc., but that it would not do while the struggle lasted to make a public claim ; " and also states that the War Power pamphlet has done much good, and he has heard it frequently referred to while in the West.

Judge Wade discusses the matter and says it greatly adds to the merit of the author that it was not made known. " Where is there another man or woman," says Judge Wade, turning to Judge Evans, " who would have kept silence when so much could have come personally from an open avowal." Judge Evans says he has reproached himself more than once that he had not in some way made known what he knew, but was constrained to silence by considerations of patriotism that were above all else at that time.

Hon. Benjamin F. Wade, Chairman of the Committee on the Conduct of the War, afterward writes to Miss Carroll :

"I have sometimes reproached myself that I had not made known the author when they were discussing the resolution in Congress to find out ; but Mr. Lincoln and Mr. Stanton were opposed to its being known that the armies were moving under the plan of a civilian. Mr. Lincoln wanted the armies to believe that they were doing the whole business of saving the country."

Mr. Wade also writes to Miss Carroll :

"The country, almost in her last extremity, was saved by your sagacity and unremitting labor ; indeed, your services were so great that it is hard to make the world believe it. That all this great work should be brought about by a woman is inconceivable to vulgar minds. You cannot be deprived of the honor of having done greater and more efficient services for the country in time of her greatest peril than any other person in the Republic, and a knowledge of this cannot be long repressed."

Col. Thomas A. Scott, Assistant Secretary of War, to whom her plans were submitted, informs her in 1862 that "the adoption of her plan has saved the country millions of money."

Hon. L. D. Evans, justice of the supreme court of Texas, in a pamphlet entitled "The Material Bearing of the Tennessee Campaign in 1862 upon the Destinies of our Civil War," shows that no military plan could have saved the country except this, and that this was unthought of and unknown until suggested by Miss Carroll, who alone had the genius to grasp the situation.

How clearly the Confederate leaders recognized the fatal

effects of this Tennessee campaign is indicated by a letter found among the papers captured by General Mitchell at Huntsville, written by General Beauregard to General Samuel Cooper, Richmond, Va. :

"CORINTH, *April 9, 1862.*

"Can we not be reinforced by Pemberton's army?" "If defeated here, we lose the Mississippi Valley and probably our cause, whereas we could even afford to lose Charleston and Savannah for the purpose of defeating Buell's army, which would not only insure us the valley of the Mississippi, but our independence."

The feeling of the Confederate army is curiously indicated by the following letter received by Miss Carroll as the struggle drew towards its close and filed by Mr. Stanton among his papers :

FORT DELAWARE, *March 1, 1865.*
MISS CARROLL, *Baltimore, Md. :*

MADAM: It is rumored in the Southern army that you furnished the plan or information that caused the United States Government to abandon the expedition designed to descend the Mississippi river, and transferred the armies up the Tennessee river in 1862. We wish to know if this is true. If it is, you are the veriest of traitors to your section, and we warn you that you stand upon a volcano.

"CONFEDERATES."

———

Miss Carroll's patriotic labors continued to the end. She contributed papers on emancipation and on reconstruction,

8 c

and wrote articles for the leading journals in support of the Government.

"While her pen was tireless in the cause of loyalty, her sympathy and interest extended themselves toward the prisons, the battlefields, and the hospitals, and many were the individual cases of suffering and want that she relieved. She was especially successful with procuring discharges for Union prisoners, and where such were in need her own means were most generously used to give adequate help."

Although the agreement with the Government was that she should be remunerated for her services and the employment of her private resources, it was not until some time after the close of the war that she endeavored, by the advice of her friends and prominent members of the War Committee, to make a public claim and establish so important a fact in the history of the war.

"Miss Carroll's own feeling was a desire to make her services a free gift to her country, and her aged father, who felt the proudest satisfaction in his daughter's patriotic career, was of the same disinterested opinion."*

The same high and chivalrous feeling that led him to sacrifice his ancestral home to liquidate the debts incurred by others made him unwilling that his daughter should press even for the payment of the debt due for the publication of her pamphlets and campaign documents, though published at the request of the War Department on the understanding that she was to be repaid. His loftiness of feeling and unbounded generosity continued even under adverse fortunes.

---

*Abbie M. Gannet, in the Boston *Sunday Herald*, February, 1890

"But as time went on, her father no longer living, Miss Carroll noted how honors and emoluments were allotted to her fellow-laborers, and that her own work, owing to the peculiar circumstances that at first surrounded it and the untimely deaths of Mr. Lincoln and others who would gladly have proclaimed it, was wholly sinking into obscurity. A sense of the injustice of the case took possession of her and the conviction that history itself would be falsified if her silence continued."*

Thomas A. Scott and Mr. Wade, chairman of the Committee on the Conduct of the War, and others well acquainted with her work were still living, able and desirous to establish her claim. By their advice and with their enthusiastic endorsement she made a statement of her case in 1870 and presented it before Congress, asking for recognition and a due award.

"Every lover of history, every true patriot, and, above all, every patriotic woman will be glad that she so decided."
—*Mrs. Abbie M. Gannet.*

It was not fitting that such achievements should be allowed to sink into oblivion.

Accordingly she made her claim, supported by the strongest and clearest testimony from the very men who were most competent to speak with absolute authority, Mr. Wade, Mr. Scott, and others of the War Department testifying again and again to the facts of the case.

It immediately became evident that a most determined effort was to be made to crush her claims. The honors of

---

* Abbie M. Gannet, in the Boston *Sunday Herald.*

war were not to be allowed to rest on the head that had so ably won them. Personal and political interests were too strongly involved. If it had been a little matter it might have passed ; but this was a case of such magnitude and importance, a case that must greatly change existing estimates.

To defeat the testimony was impossible. Other means must be used. Chicanery of every kind was resorted to.

Twice Miss Carroll's whole file of papers were stolen from the Military Committee, who were considering her claims.

Fortunately Miss Carroll possessed the original drafts of these letters. She speedily reproduced them, and the Military Committee and Mr. Hunt, the keeper of the records, having already examined the letters, accepted the new file and ordered them to be printed, thus giving them their guarantee ; so that, to all intents and purposes, they became the same as the originals.

Judge Wade advises Miss Carroll :

" I want you to set forth to these gentlemen, in your private letters, the facts about the abstracting of these papers. It has never been properly done. It is exceedingly important as evidence of the truth of your claim. Tell them how your papers were abstracted from the files twice. Send a letter to General Banning. Tell Judge Evans to ask the General to appoint a sub-committee to investigate it, so as to submit it to the general committee. Tell them all, and remind them that when one report was made in the Senate Committee by Mr. Howard the papers were abstracted from the files, as the Secretary of the Committee, Rev. Samuel Hunt, will testify. I hope the report will be a very emphatic and explicit one in setting forth your plan as you took it to Colonel Scott. It makes the strongest foundation to commence upon in the sub-committee. There will undoubtedly be a minority of Republicans, and it will be so much the better for that, because they can find no evidence to invalidate the report of the majority, and I would like to see them make the attempt. Being at the head of the War Committee, I had most to do with it. The committee not half the time were present. Nobody knows the difficulty the War Committee had to get the army moved. We had almost to fight for that campaign."

Mr. Hunt writes from Natick, Mass.:

March 7, 1876.

MY DEAR MISS CARROLL:

I remember well your failure to recover twice all the papers you intrusted to the charge of the Military Committee and our inability to account for their loss.

Hoping you will have better success now, I remain as ever,
    Very truly yours,

S. HUNT,
Late Secretary of Senate Military Committee.

Senator Howard tells Miss Carroll she has a right to feel disappointed that her claims should be neglected, but he says, "you know the great power of the *military*, who don't want you to have the recognition."

"Senator Howard," she replies, "there is something in

moral integrity. I understand you, but just tell the *truth*. I ask only to be sustained by truth, and am not afraid of this power.''

"Miss Carroll," he says with emphasis, " you have done more for the country than them all. You told and showed where to fight and how to strike the rebellion upon its head. No one comprehends the magnitude of that service more than I.''

Judge Wade's remarks to Senator Wilson last of May, 1862 (as taken down by a reporter):

Judge Wade said he talked just right to Wilson for the delay in Miss Carroll's matter before his committee ; that Wilson said he was no more against the claim than Wade. Wade told him it would *kill* him politically if he didn't act soon ; that it ought to kill any party who knew the truths of the great civil war and conspired to conceal them for their own purposes ; that it would be a great feather in a man's cap and a great help to his own cause to bring the matter before the country *right*, no matter *who* it offended, and he only regretted he was not in the Senate then on this very account, and would always be sorry he had not induced Miss Carroll to come out and make claim for her rights while the rejoicing was going on at the final surrender. Wilson said it was a big thing, and he agreed that the American people would cheerfully pay for it, if it had been so done, by contribution boxes at the cross-roads and post-offices of the country.

Mr. Tucker writes from Philadelphia in 1870:

" I saw Colonel Scott yesterday and placed your papers in his hands. He remarked that he should stand by all he had said or written in the matter, and he presumed that was all you would want."

1872.

Judge Wade says : " I went to Morton, in the Senate, and told him that it was infamous that the Military Committee did not report at once. He said, for himself he was ready to endorse your claim fully, and had done so when Howard reported. I went on to tell him more, but he said, ' I could not be more strongly convinced of the justice of that claim. Your own statement satisfied me without anything more. If Wilson will send down for the report I will sign my name to it right now.' I then went over to Wilson and told him what Morton had said, and told him he had better send down for it. Wilson said he didn't think that was the best way of doing it, but that he would call a special meeting of the Committee and have it done. I then saw Cameron. He said he was ready and always had been."

1873.

Judge Wade tells her : " Howe said your claim had been sent to his committee—on Claims—but that it did not properly belong there ; but that he had examined the papers ; that your claim was entirely just and ought to be paid."

And again : " That he had spoken to Wadleigh, a member of the Military Committee, about her claim. He said he had no question that it was clearly proved, and no doubt she would be ultimately paid by the Government."

1874.

Judge Wade says : " I asked Logan what he was going to do about Miss Carroll's claim." He said " he didn't know what to say." " I told him it ought to be paid at once ; that it was clearly established." Logan said, " Yes ; but she claims so much." Wade replies, " She claims to have furnished the information that led to the military movements that decided the war." Logan didn't say any more, or what he would do.

Judge Wade asked Morrill what he was going to do ; that this claim had been before Congress long enough. Morrill said your claim was clearly established ; "that were you applying for a title for a new patent of discovery nothing could defeat you, but that it was indispensable to have the Military Committee act again." Wade says "he feels embarrassed in appearing as an advocate, being a witness, but that he will go before the committee anyhow and insist upon action."

JEFFERSON, OHIO, *October 3, 1876.*

MY DEAR MISS CARROLL :

I do assure you that the manner in which your most noble services and sacrifices have been treated by your country has given me more pain and anxiety than anything that ever happened to me personally ; that such merit should go so long unrewarded is deeply disgraceful to the country, or rather to the agencies of the Government who have had the matter in charge. I hope and trust it will not always be so. The truth is, your services were so great they cannot be comprehended by the ordinary capacity of our public men ; and then, again, your services were of such a character that they threw a shadow over the reputations of some of our would-be great men. No doubt great pains have been taken in the business of trying to defeat you, but it has always been an article of faith with me that truth and justice must ultimately triumph.

Ever yours truly,

B. F. WADE.

JEFFERSON, OHIO, *April 10, 1877.*

MY DEAR MISS CARROLL:

There is nothing in my power I would not most gladly do for you, for none have ever done so much for the country as you, and none have had so little for it. I cannot but believe justice will be done you yet for the immense services you rendered the country in the civil war. But when I reflect what mighty work you have done for the country and how you have been treated it keeps me awake nights and fills my soul with bitterness.

Truly yours ever,

B. F. WADE.

JEFFERSON, OHIO, *September 4, 1877.*

MY DEAR MISS CARROLL:

* * * I know you are right and I will never fail to do all I can to aid you in attaining it. Your only trouble is you have the whole army to fight, who seem better skilled in opposing you than they were in finding out the best method of fighting the enemy. I hope your health holds out and continues good, for what you have done and what you have to do would break down any weaker intellect and physical constitution.

Mrs. Wade joins me in wishing you all success.

Truly yours,

B. F. WADE.

Governor Corwin writes her:

WASHINGTON, *Jan. 13, 1878.*

DEAR FRIEND:

I thank you for the address of your good Governor of the third instant. I believe you will succeed in saving Maryland, but there is nothing to be done with this Congress, and your counsel to your friends is wise. Art, finesse, and trick are in this age worth the wisdom of Solomon, the faith of Abraham, and the fidelity of Moses.

Truly yours,

TOM CORWIN.*

Soon after the close of the war Miss Carroll inquires of Mr. Stanton if he could not furnish what was termed "a transportation and subsistence" for a southern tour. Many people were present. He remarks he had rather pay her millions of dollars than to say no to any request she could make of him. "You," he says, "who have done such incomparable services for the country with so much modesty and so little pretension," etc.

Miss Carroll does not like so much in the line of compliment and says to General Hardie as she passes out, "Mr. Stanton said too much and attracted the attention of all in the room."

Hardie says, "Don't take it in that light. Mr. Stanton is not the man to say what he don't mean, and, I venture to say, never said so much to any one besides during the war."

----

* Thomas Corwin was Secretary of the Treasury under Fillmore, U. S. Senator, a noted lawyer and wit, and a man of letters.

Miss Carroll relates this to Judge Wade.   " Why," says he, " Stanton has said the same of you to me, and often in the same vein ; he said your course was the most remarkable in the war ; that you found yourself, got no pay, and did the great work that made others famous.''

For these reports and conversations see—

45th CONGRESS, } HOUSE OF REPRESENTATIVES. } MISS. DOC.
  2nd SESSION. }   Pp. 30, 31, 32, 33.   }   No. 58.

Vol. 6, Miscellaneous Documents, Document Room of the Senate.

CHAPTER VII.

In July of 1862 Miss Carroll presented her very modest bill for the pamphlets that had been accepted at the War Department, which included the expenses paid by herself of printing and circulating.

Of the Breckenridge pamphlet she printed and circulated 50,000, which went off, as Hon. James Tilghman (president of the Union Association in Baltimore in 1860) testifies, "like hot cakes."

In the library of the State Department specimens of two large editions of the War Powers may be seen side by side in the volumes of bound manuscripts. It is over 23 closely printed pages in length, and was circulated east and west with admirable results, all expenses borne by Miss Carroll personally.

The Power of the President to Suspend the Writ of *Habeas Corpus*, The Relation of the Revolted Citizens to the United States, and other able papers followed.

The Secretary of War suggested the presentation of Miss Carroll's bill, advising her to obtain the opinion of one or more competent judges as to the reasonableness of her charges and a statement of the understanding upon which they were written.

The bill is as follows, and the testimonials are as reported in the Miss. Doc. 58 (House), 45th Congress, 2d session :

Secret-Service **Fund of the War** *Department to Anna Ella* **Carroll, Dr.,** *as* **per** *Agreement with Hon.* **Thomas A. Scott, Assistant** *Secretary of War.*

1861.

Sept. 25.	To circulating the Breckenridge reply . .	$1,250
Dec. 24.	To writing, publishing, and circulating the "War Powers," etc.	3,000
1862.		
May —.	Writing, publishing, and circulating the relations of the National Government to the rebelled citizens	2,000
		$6,250
Credit, October 2, 1861 :		
By cash		1,250
		$5,000

PHILADELPHIA, *January 2, 1863.*

I believe Miss Carroll has earned fairly, and should be paid, the compensation she has charged above.

THOS. A. SCOTT.

PHILADELPHIA, *January 28, 1863.*

All my interviews with Miss Carroll were in my official capacity as Assistant Secretary of War, and in that capacity I would have allowed, and believed she should be paid, the amount of her bill within, which is certified as being reasonable by many of the leading men of the country.

THOS. A. SCOTT.

PHILADELPHIA, *January 28, 1863.*

The pamphlets published by Miss Carroll were published upon a general understanding made by me with her as Assistant Secretary of War, under no special authority in the premises, but under a general authority then exercised by me in the discharge of public duties as Assistant Secretary of War. I then thought them of value to the service, and still believe they were of great value to the Government. I brought the matter generally to the knowledge of General Cameron, then Secretary of War, without his having special knowledge of the whole matter ; he made no objections thereto. No price was fixed, but it was understood that the Government would treat her with sufficient liberality to compensate her for any service she might render, and I believe she acted upon the expectation that she would be paid by the Government.

THOMAS A. SCOTT.

NEW YORK, *October 10, 1862.*

Without intending to express any assent or dissent to the positions therein asserted, but merely with a view of forming a judgment in respect to their merits as argumentative compositions, I have carefully perused Miss Carroll's pamphlets mentioned in the within account. The propositions are clearly stated, the authorities relied on are judiciously selected, and the reasoning is natural, direct, and well sustained, and framed in a manner extremely well adapted to win the reader's assent, and thus to obtain the object in view. I consider the charges quite moderate.

CHARLES O'CONOR.

WASHINGTON, *September 19, 1862.*

Without having seen the writings mentioned in the within account I have heard them so favorably spoken of by the

most competent judges that the charges of the account seem
to be most reasonable.

REVERDY JOHNSON.

---

706 WALNUT ST., PHILADELPHIA, *Oct. 11, 1862.*

Having been requested to give my opinion of the pamphlets described in the within list, I have in a cursory way
looked over them. As I have just returned from Europe
from a long absence and am at present with many unsettled
matters of my own, I cannot undertake therefore to study
them. From the examination I have given them I cheerfully say they appear to be learned and able productions
and the work of a well-stored mind. They are written in
a clear style and must be read with interest and advantage,
and certainly cannot fail to be of service to the cause they
uphold.

Much labor must have been given to these productions.
Their actual value in money I cannot determine, but I
think they are well worthy of a high and liberal compensation.

BENJAMIN H. BREWSTER.*

WASHINGTON, *September 23, 1862.*

I have read several of the productions of Miss Carroll,
and, among others, two of the within mentioned. The
learning, ability, and force of reasoning they exhibit have
astonished me. Without concurring in all the conclusions
of the writer, I think that the writer is fully entitled, not
only to the amount charged, but to the thanks and high
consideration of the Government and the nation.

RICHARD S. COXE.

---

* Benjamin H. Brewster was a noted lawyer of Philadelphia and a member
of Arthur's Cabinet.

WASHINGTON, *September 10, 1862.*

Having read with care the several pamphlets mentioned within, and comparing them with professional arguments in causes of any considerable importance, and considering the vast learning and the ability with which it is handled, I have to say that in my judgment the charges are not only very reasonable, but will, in the estimation of all men of learning who will carefully examine the documents, be deemed *too small.*

L. D. EVANS.

WASHINGTON, D. C., *September 23, 1862.*

I have read the pamphlets mentioned within, together with others on similar subjects written by Miss Carroll, and I fully concur in the opinion above expressed, believing that said pamphlets have been of essential service to the cause of the Union.

S. T. WILLIAMS.

September 8, 1862.

I have carefully perused, some time since, the papers referred to within, and without entering into any question of concurrence or non-concurrence of views I deem the documents of great value to the Government, and that the estimate of the account is reasonable.

ROBERT J. WALKER.

WASHINGTON, *October, 1862.*

MISS CARROLL:

While I never put my name to any paper, I would very cheerfully state at the Department that I consider the charges for your publications *too small,* but I do not think it can be necessary. What more could any one want than such an endorsement as you have from Mr. O'Conor and other eminent men ?

Very respectfully,

EDWARDS PIERREPONT.*

Later developments showed that the $1,250 that Miss Carroll had credited to the secret-service fund had come out of Thomas A. Scott's own pocket as his private contribution to the national cause and to help on the circulation of such important documents.

Mr. Scott sent the following letter, to be found in Miss. Doc. 167 :

PHILADELPHIA, *January 16, 1863.*

Hon. JOHN TUCKER, *Assistant Secretary of War :*

I believe Miss Carroll has fairly earned and ought to be paid the amount of her bill ($6,750), and if you will pay her I will certify to such form as you may think necessary as a voucher.

THOMAS A. SCOTT.

Mr. Tucker not having the settlement of the account, and the matter being referred to Assistant Secretary Watson, Miss Carroll submitted the account endorsed by many eminent men as reasonable, and also endorsed with Hon. Thomas A. Scott's recollection of the agreement upon which they were produced.

An agent tendered but $750, *with a receipt in full.*

On objecting he said her redress was with Congress, and,

---

* Edwards Pierrepont was Minister to England under Grant.

9 C

upon being informed by Mr. Reverdy Johnson that the receipts would not bar her claim, she accepted it.   The original account, with endorsements, etc., it is stated, is "on file in the War Department."   The Senate Military Com. mittee of the 41st Congress, 3d session, Report 339, referring to these publications, said : "Miss Carroll preferred a claim to reimburse her for expenses incurred in their publication which ought to have been paid."

Miss Carroll having also credited the $750 to the secret-service fund, Mr. Thomas A. Scott wrote her that she should not have done so ; that it came out of his own pocket in his indignation at finding the agreement made by himself in his capacity of Assistant Secretary of War disregarded by his successor.   For thirty years this account has been presented in vain.   In 1885 it was retransmitted from the Court of Claims on some judicial grounds, though accompanied by the "moral assent" of the court.

Miss Carroll had written the great and influential pamphlets of the day which ought to have made her a minister of state.   She had devised the military movements that ought to have given her a very high military rank.   Under our arrangements for securing a male aristocracy no services, however brilliant, could secure to a woman any post whatever.   She must remain an *unrecognized* member, and being an unrecognized member for her there was no pay— not even her traveling expenses.   Any help towards the circulation of her invaluable pamphlets had to come out of the private means of Thomas A. Scott.   From first to last, for all her intense and unremitting labors through all the years of the civil war, she has, it would appear, received from the *Government*, in any department whatever, not one cent. To her personally, through the generous and unhesitating use of her own private means, the result has been a long martyrdom of poverty and suffering.

That is how America has treated her noblest daughter.

That is the result of belonging to a disfranchised class.

CHAPTER VIII.

Miss Carroll's first memorial was brought before Congress March 31, 1870. It was simple and short, with a copy of the plan of campaign appended.

A Military Committee, with General Jacob M. Howard as chairman, was appointed to consider it. Thomas A. Scott wrote twice to the Military Committee endorsing the claim. Mr. Wade, Judge Evans, etc., made their statements on affidavit.

The evidence being thorough and incontrovertible, Mr. Howard reported accordingly on February 2, 1871. He recapitulates the letters and evidence received; gives Mr. Wade's testimony; states that a copy of Miss Carroll's paper was shown him immediately after the success of the campaign, by the late Hon. Elisha Whittlesey,* of Ohio (Mr. Whittlesey had asked Miss Carroll for a copy that he might leave it in his family as an heirloom); notes Miss Carroll's statement that no military man had ever controverted her claim to having originated the campaign, and concludes:

" From the high social position of this lady and her established ability as a writer and thinker, she was prepared

---

* Elisha Whittlesey was Comptroller of the Treasury at the time of his death, a very distinguished lawyer in Ohio, and for many terms a Representative in Congress.

(132)

at the inception of the rebellion to exercise a strong influence in behalf of liberty and the Union ; that it was felt and respected in Maryland during the darkest hours in that State's history, there can be no question.   Her publications throughout the struggle were eloquently and ably written and widely circulated, and did much to arouse and invigorate the sentiment of loyalty in Maryland and other border States.   It is not too much to say that they were among the very ablest publications of the time and exerted a powerful influence upon the hearts of the people.   Some of these publications were prepared under the auspices of the War Department, and for these Miss Carroll preferred a claim to reimburse her for the expenses incurred in their publication, which ought to have been paid ; and, as evidence of this, we subjoin the following statement from the Assistant Secretary of War :—

"'PHILADELPHIA, *January 28, 1863.*

"'All my interviews with Miss Carroll were in my official capacity as Assistant Secretary of War.   The pamphlets published were, to a certain extent, under a general authority then exercised by me in the discharge of public duties as Assistant Secretary of War.   No price was fixed, but it was understood that the Government would 'treat her with sufficient liberality to compensate her for any service she might render.' "

On the fifteenth of June, 1870, Hon. Thomas A. Scott addressed a letter to Hon. J. M. Howard, U. S. Senate, in which he says :

" ' I learn from Miss Carroll that she has a claim before Congress for services rendered in the year 1861 in aid of the Government. I believe now that the Government ought to reward her liberally for the efforts she made in its behalf to rouse the people against the rebellious action of the South. I hope you will pass some measure that will give Miss Carroll what she is certainly entitled to.

" ' Thos. A. Scott.' "

" In view, therefore, of the highly meritorious services of Miss Carroll during the whole period of our National troubles, and especially at that epoch of the war to which her memorial makes reference, and in consideration of the further fact that all the expenses incident to this service were borne by herself, the committee believe her claim to be just, and that it ought to be recognized by Congress, and consequently report a bill for her relief."

An accompanying bill was sent in, leaving the amount of compensation blank for Congress to determine, but the committee agreeing that the bill ought to be passed in some manner that should recognize the remarkable and invaluable nature of the services rendered.

Congress having thus received the report made by their own Military Committee appointed for the purpose, for reasons plainly given by Mr. Wade and others, at once ignored it, tossing it over to the Court of Claims, who would have nothing to do with it, and so that Congress adjourned.

Then followed that singular and disheartening feature of congressional committees.

Action having been taken, a Military Committee appointed, and a conclusive report made, Congress could utterly neglect it, and at the following Congress the previous action would count for nothing, and the whole wearisome proceeding of a new memorial, a new effort to procure attention, a new examination of evidence, a new report, a new bill, and again utter neglect. But the brave woman continued. She was really fighting alone and at terrible odds another Tennessee campaign for the rightful recognition of woman's work.

Accordingly, the following year another memorial was sent in, another committee appointed, renewed testimony given by Scott, Wade, Evans, and others. Mr. Wilson testified that the claim was " incontestably established," referred to the evidence given in Miss Carroll's own memorial, but for want of time made no regular report, apparently, except this :

Report.

" Mr. Wilson, on behalf of the Committee on Military Affairs, laid before the Senate the memorial of Anna Ella Carroll, of Maryland, setting forth certain valuable military information given to the Government by her during the war and asking compensation therefor, which was ordered to be printed, together with a bill rewarding her for military and literary services "—twice read in United States Senate— amount left $—, to be filled by this body. Then Congress again quietly dropped a recognition that might interfere with party plans, and so *that* Congress adjourned.

And so the weary work went on of presenting new memorials and meeting with the same neglect, Congress never denying the claim and none of the military commanders making any claim or denying the facts.

Miss Carroll gave extracts from every known historical work showing the surmises made, endeavoring to attribute the plan to one and another, and no evidence found to establish such surmises.

Miss Carroll wrote to Hon. J. T. Headley, the distinguished historian of the Civil War, and received the following letter :

NEWBURGH, N. Y., *February 6, 1873.*

MY DEAR MADAM :

I am much obliged for the pamphlet you sent me. I never knew before with whom the plan of the campaign up the Tennessee river originated. There seemed to be a mystery attached to it that I could not solve. Though General Buell sent me an immense amount of documents relating to this campaign I could find no reference to the origin of the change of plan. Afterwards I saw it attributed to Halleck, which I knew to be false, and I noticed that he never corroborated it. It is strange that after all my research it has rested with you to enlighten me.

Money cannot pay for the plan of that campaign. I doubt not Congress will show not liberality but some justice in the matter.

Yours very sincerely,

J. T. HEADLEY.

So matters went on. New memorials presented for the most part met with " leave to withdraw." Then Miss Carroll gathered herself up for a supreme effort, presented fresh testimony, and in 1878 sent in a memorial that is a mine of wealth and the most interesting memorial she has ever presented. It is labeled—

45th CONGRESS, } HOUSE OF REPRESENTATIVES. { MISS. DOC.
2d SESSION.   No. 58.

Being a document of the first importance and containing some singular evidence, it has been systematically excluded from every Congressional index, though published by order of Congress and included in the bound volumes.

Miss Carroll having made in 1878 this very notable memorial, on February 18, 1879—

45th CONGRESS, } SENATE { REPORT
3d SESSION.   No. 775.

Mr. Cockrell made a report entered on the Congressional lists as *adverse,* but really an additional evidence of the incontrovertible nature of the facts and the testimony of the case, the report being only adverse as to compensation. The report admits the services, both literary and military, and even concedes the proposition that "*the transfer of the national armies from the banks of the Ohio up the Tennessee river to the decisive position in Mississippi was the greatest military event in the interest of the human race known to modern ages, and will ever rank among the very few strategic movements in the world's history that have decided the fate of empires and peoples,*" and that "*no true history can be written that does not assign to the memorialist the credit of the conception.*"

The report thereupon proceeds to state the opinion of the committee, that with all the evidence before them every subsequent Congress having failed to make an award they must have had some unknown reasons for the omission, and that the claim, having been so long neglected, may as well be indefinitely postponed—a surprising mode of reasoning and manner of disposition of a claim.

The report supposes the neglect was due to the fact that the services were rendered to the Secret Service Commission and inclines to think that the two thousand dollars received was considered a sufficient remuneration for the literary work.

"The committee have not been able to find a precedent for payment of claims of this character." * * * "But it would destroy much of the poetry and grandeur of noble deeds were a price demanded for kindred services, and achievements of this nature huckstered in the market as commodities of barter." *And that is all a report intended to be adverse can say against the claim.*

One might remark that it is not wholly unprecedented for honorable gentlemen to receive remuneration from the Government for services rendered, or even to ask for their traveling expenses. But this looks somewhat like a sneer.

Was it directed against the noble invalid who had devoted her life and strength, her great ability, and her private fortune to the service of her country for years, with such lavish prodigality and such brilliant success, and had left a fitting award wholly to the determination of Congress, asking only that it should be made in some way that should mark the unusual and distinctive nature of the services rendered?

No ; surely it must have been directed against the Government agent who wanted Miss Carroll, for the consideration of $750, to give a receipt in full for a bill of $5,000 remaining—a bill certified by the highest authorities to be sufficiently low or altogether *too* low for the literary work performed. (No wonder if *such* huckstering moved Mr. Cockrell's righteous soul.) His remarks also were exceedingly applicable to a liberal-minded person who shortly after sent in a bill recommending that after all these years Congress would kindly allow Miss Carroll a pension of *$50 a month* for "the important military services rendered the country by her during the late civil war." If any more $50 miseries are proposed we would commend to the committees Mr. Cockrell on "huckstering."

The true description of such a report would be "admission of the incontestable nature of the services rendered."

Then followed the report of the Military Committee of 1881—the last report, so far as I have been able to ascertain, "printed by order of Congress."

It is as follows, *verbatim :*

46th CONGRESS, 3d SESSION. } HOUSE OF REPRESENTATIVES. { REPORT No. 386.

ANNA ELLA CARROLL.

March 3, 1881.—Committed to the Committee of the Whole House and ordered to be printed.

E. S. Bragg, from the Committee on Military Affairs, submitted the following

Report.

(To accompany bill H. R. 7256.)

The Committee on Military Affairs, to whom the memorial of Anna Ella Carroll was referred, asking national recognition and reward for services rendered the United States during the war between the States, after careful consideration of the same, submit the following :

In the autumn of 1861 the great question as to whether the Union could be saved, or whether it was hopelessly subverted, depended on the ability of the Government to open the Mississippi and deliver a fatal blow upon the resources of the Confederate power.

The original plan was to reduce the formidable fortifications by descending this river aided by the gunboat fleet then in preparation for that object.

President Lincoln had reserved to himself the special direction of this expedition, but before it was prepared to move he became convinced that the obstacles to be encountered were too grave and serious for the success which the exigencies of the crisis demanded, and the plan was then abandoned and the armies diverted up the Tennessee river and thence southward to the center of the Confederate power.

The evidence before this committee completely establishes that Miss Anna Ella Carroll was the author of this change of plan, which involved a transfer of the national forces to

their new base in north Mississippi and Alabama, in command of the Memphis and Charleston railroad. That she
devoted time and money in the autumn of 1861 to the investigation of its feasability is established by the sworn testimony of L. D. Evans, chief justice of the supreme court
of Texas, to the Military Committee of the United States
Senate in the 42d Congress (see pp. 40, 41 of the memorial); that after that investigation she submitted her plan
in writing to the War Department at Washington, placing
it in the hands of Col. Thomas A. Scott, Assistant Secretary of War, as is confirmed by his statement (see p. 38 of
the memorial); also confirmed by the statement of Hon. B.
F. Wade, chairman of the Committee on the Conduct of
the War, made to the same committee (see p. 38), and of
President Lincoln and Secretary Stanton (see p. 39 of memorial); also by Hon. O. H. Browning, of Illinois, Senator
during the war, in confidential relations with President Lincoln and Secretary Stanton (see p. 39 of memorial); also
that of Hon. Elisha Whittlesey, Comptroller of the Treasury
(see p. 41 of memorial); also by Hon. Thomas H. Hicks,
Governor of Maryland, and by Hon. Frederick Feckey's
affidavit, Comptroller of the Public Works of Maryland
(see p. 127 of memorial); by Hon. Reverdy Johnson (see
pp. 26 and 41 of memorial); Hon. George Vickers, United
States Senator from Maryland (see p. 41 of memorial); again
by Hon. B. F. Wade (see p. 41 of memorial); Hon. J. T.
Headley (see p. 43 of memorial); Rev. Dr. R. J. Breckenridge on services (see p. 47 of memorial); Prof. Joseph
Henry, Rev. Dr. Hodge, of theological seminary at Prince-

ton (see p. 30 of memorial) ; remarkable interviews and correspondence of Judge B. F. Wade (see pp. 23-26 of memorial).

That this campaign prevented the recognition of Southern independence by its fatal effects on the Confederate States is shown by letters from Hon. C. M. Clay (see pp. 40, 43 of memorial), and by his letters from St. Petersburgh ; also those of Mr. Adams and Mr. Dayton from London and Paris (see pp. 100-102 of memorial).

That the campaign defeated national bankruptcy, then imminent, and opened the way for a system of finance to defend the Federal cause is shown by the debates of the period in both Houses of Congress ; by the utterances of Mr. Spalding, Mr. Diven, Mr. Thaddeus Stevens, Mr. Roscoe Conkling, Mr. John Sherman, Mr. Henry Wilson, Mr. Fessenden, Mr. Trumbull, Mr. Foster, Mr. Garrett Davis, Mr. John C. Crittenden, &c., found for convenient reference in appendix to memorial, page 59 ; also therein the opinion of the English press as to why the Union could not be restored.

The condition of the struggle can best be realized as depicted by the leading statesmen in Congress previous to the execution of these military movements (see synopsis of debates from *Congressional Globe*, pp. 21, 22 of memorial).

The effect of this campaign upon the country and the anxiety to find out and reward the author are evinced by the resolution of Mr. Roscoe Conkling in the House or Representatives, 24th of February, 1862 (see debates on the origin of the campaign, pp. 39-63 of memorial). But it was deemed prudent to make no public claim as to authorship while the war lasted (see Colonel Scott's view, p. 32 of memorial).

The wisdom of the plan was proven, not only by the absolute advantages which resulted, giving the mastery of the conflict to the national arms and ever more assuring their success even against the powers of all Europe should they have combined, but it was likewise proven by the failures to open the Mississippi or win any decided success on the plan first devised by the Government.

It is further conclusively shown that no plan, order, letter, telegram, or suggestion of the Tennessee river as the line of invasion has ever been produced except in the paper submitted by Miss Carroll on the 30th of November, 1861, and her subsequent letters to the Government as the campaign progressed.

It is further shown to this committee that the able and patriotic publications of the memorialist in pamphlets and newspapers, with her high social influence, not only largely contributed to the cause of the Union in her own State, Maryland (see Governor Hicks' letters, p. 27 of memorial), but exerted a wide and salutary influence on all the border States (see Howard's Report, p. 33, and p. 75 of memorial).

These publications were used by the Government as war measures, and the debate in Congress shows that she was the first writer on the war powers of the Government (see p. 45 of memorial). Leading statesmen and jurists bore testimony to their value, including President Lincoln, Secretaries Chase, Stanton, Seward, Welles, Smith, Attorney

General Bates, Senators Browning, Doolittle, Collamer, Cowan, Reverdy Johnson, and Hicks, Hon. Horace Binney, Hon. Benjamin H. Brewster, Hon. William M. Meredith, Hon. Robert J. Walker, Hon. Charles O'Connor, Hon. Edwards Pierrepont, Hon. Edward Everett, Hon. Thomas Corwin, Hon. Francis Thomas, of Maryland, and many others, found in memorial.

The Military Committee, through General Howard, in the Forty-first Congress, 3d session, Document No. 337, unanimously reported that Miss Carroll did cause the change of the military expedition from the Mississippi to the Tennessee, &c. ; and the aforesaid act of the 42d Congress, 2d session, Document No. 167, as found in memorial, reported through Hon. Henry Wilson the evidence and bill in support of this claim.   Again, in the Forty-fourth Congress, the Military Committee of the House favorably considered this claim, and Gen. A. S. Williams was prepared to report, and, being prevented by want of time, placed on record that this claim is incontestably established, and that the country owes to Miss Carroll a large and honest compensation, both in money and in honors, for her services in the national crises.

In view of all these facts, this committee believes that the thanks of the nation are due Miss Carroll, and that they are fully justified in recommending that she be placed on the pension rolls of the Government as a partial measure of recognition for her public service, and report herewith a bill for such purpose and recommend its passage.

Hon. E. M. Stanton came into the War Department in 1862 pledged to execute the Tennessee campaign.

Statement from Hon. B. F. Wade, chairman of the Committee on the Conduct of the War, April 4, 1876. (This is the long letter from Mr. Wade, which we have already given, and we need not repeat it.)

General Bragg prepared and suggested the following bill to accompany the report :

* "*Be it enacted*, That the same sum and emoluments given by the Government to the major generals of the United States Army be paid to Anna Ella Carroll from the date of her services to the country, in November, 1861, to the time of the passage of this act ; and the further payment of the same amount as the pay and emoluments of a major general of the United States Army be paid to her in quarterly installments to the end of her life, as a partial measure of recognition of her services to the nation," and recommend its passage.

To suggest a bill that should rightfully mark the pre-eminently military nature of the services rendered without giving offense to the class accustomed to monopolize the sounding titles and to wear the glittering plumes was a wonderfully difficult thing to do. Here at least was a brave and honest effort to accomplish what no previous committee had even attempted. The other committees

---

* I copied this from a printed account some years ago. Conversing lately with a friend of General Bragg, I was assured that this was the first bill prepared.

10 C

had left the award a blank, to be filled in by a puzzled and unwilling Congress, who preferred to do nothing at all.

In England probably there would not have been the same insuperable difficulty, a sovereign lady holding high military office as a matter of course ; but we have thrown aside some noble traditions, and America never has a sovereign lady.

There was something noble and fitting in this recommendation of award by General Bragg. Considering how great public services have been formerly rewarded, it was certainly not extreme.

To go back to English history :

" The Duke of Marlborough, who commanded the allied armies of England, Austria, and Germany, received the most flattering testimonials in all forms. A principality was voted to him in Germany, while the English Government settled upon him the manor of Woodstock, long a royal residence, and erected thereon a magnificent palace as an expression of a nation's gratitude. On the Duke of Wellington honors, offices, and rewards were showered from every quarter. The crown exhausted its stores of titles, and in addition to former grants the sum of £200,000 was voted in 1815 for the purchase of a mansion and estate, etc. The rank of field marshal in four of the greatest armies in the world was bestowed by the leading governments of Europe.

" In England it has for a long time been the custom to reward and honor those illustrious in the realms of science and literature as well as of military success. Though with less demonstration and expenditure of wealth, our own country has not overlooked signal services in its behalf. The government of Pennsylvania in the days of the Revolution voted £2,500 for the political writings of Thomas Paine, and New York a farm of 300 acres in a high state of cultivation, with elegant and spacious buildings. Washington himself gave a woman a sergeant's commission in the army, who stood at the gun by which her husband had fallen, and on his recommendation she was placed on the pay-roll for life.

"Congress, in pursuance of this feeling, has not been unmindful of Anderson's heroic defense of Fort Sumter, of Farragut's capture of New Orleans, of Rawlins, etc., of Stanton, and of Lincoln, in conferring tokens of recognition for their services upon the families who survived them. Many instances might be cited where public-spirited women have been rewarded for services rendered in individual cases during the late struggle and in other forms since."

And was it not fitting that the author of such influential pamphlets and the designer of the remarkable plan of the Tennessee campaign should be honorably recognized and rewarded?

Miss Carroll was in her 66th year at the time of General Bragg's recommendation. Her father was no longer living, her family was scattered, her health was failing, and her time, strength, and fortune had been wholly expended in the service of her country with noble generosity and the most brilliant results. Surely she deserved to spend the remaining years of her life in honorable independence, distinguished and beloved by the nation to whom she had rendered incalculable service.

Now it seemed as if, after such an unqualified indorsement of her work by three successive military committees appointed for the purpose, and a suitable bill prepared, that surely her cause was won.   Miss Carroll had been informed of the report and of the bill that had been prepared.   But the Military Committee, having made this excellent summary of evidence, indorsed Miss Carroll's claim in the strongest manner, and prepared a noble and fitting bill, became greatly alarmed at what they had done.   Leaving their report unchanged, at the last moment they hastily withdrew the dignified and fitting bill and substituted in its place the following surprising performance :

"*Be it enacted by the Senate and House of Representatives of the United States of America in Congress assembled*, That the Secretary of the Interior be, and he is hereby, authorized and directed to place upon the pension-rolls of the United States the name of Anna Ella Carroll, and to pay to her a pension of fifty dollars per month from and after the passage of this act, during her life, for the important military service rendered the country by her during the late civil war."

Such a report and *such* a bill side by side stand an anomaly unparalleled.

Truly the life of the nation was rated as a cheap thing.

Of course the bill died immediately of its own glaring and ineffable meanness.

One can hardly say whether it would have been the more

unworthy thing to pass such a bill or to pass none at all ; but the last, being the most timorous course, had been adopted for ten successive years, as it has also been resorted to in the ten succeeding ones.

The Military Committee of 1881, having accomplished this astonishing feat, threw away their arms and ignominiously fled—and Congress followed in the rear, indefinitely postponing action on an unwelcome claim, that always *would* turn up "incontestably proven."

CHAPTER IX.

A WOUNDED VETERAN RETIRES FROM THE FIELD—INTER-
VIEW WITH GRANT—THE WOMEN OF AMERICA MAKE THE
CAUSE THEIR OWN—A NATIONAL LESSON.

Miss Carroll, urged on by the friends of justice and historical verity, had made great efforts rightly to present her
case and to get together a wonderful mass of indubitable
testimony.

She had been informed of the thorough endorsement of
her claim made by the Military Committee and reported by
General Bragg, and of the noble and fitting bill which he
had prepared. Then came that pitiful little bill and the
adjournment of Congress without taking further action
upon the claim.

She perhaps did not realize, in the presence of what seemed
immediate defeat, that she had performed a great and lasting
historical work in putting the whole matter on immovable
record ; but she certainly realized that, though an angel
should come from heaven to testify, it would be useless to
expect national recognition. A reaction of discourage-
ment followed, and she was suddenly stricken down by
paralysis, which threatened at once to terminate her noble
life. For three years she hovered between life and death,
no hope being entertained of her recovery. Then the
natural vigor of her constitution reasserted itself, and she

slowly regained a very considerable portion of health ; but any subsequent efforts with regard to her claim, though receiving her assent, had to be made without her personal co-operation, as mental fatigue was imperatively forbidden. She had ceased to hope for any benefit to herself personally from the prosecution of her claim ; but, rejoicing in the sense of the great work that she had been providentially called upon to accomplish, she rested in the serene conviction that with the incontestable evidence that had been presented the facts could not be forever buried out of sight, and that ultimately the truths of history would be secure.

When Miss Carroll, who had hitherto been as a tower of strength to her family, was suddenly stricken down, fortune seemed to be at its lowest ebb ; but again the Carroll energy and ability came to the rescue. An unmarried sister, with noble devotion, sustained the nation's benefactress. She obtained work in teaching in Baltimore and by hard daily toil provided for her support. But those were very dark days that followed. Then this same brave sister, through the influence of an eminent lady at the White House, obtained a clerkship at the Treasury, at Washington, brought her sister from Baltimore and established her in a little unpretending family home, which she has sustained to this day.

NOTE.—Owing to the confusion attendant upon Miss Carroll's well-nigh fatal illness and her subsequent removal to Baltimore, a trunk and box marked A. E. C. were left behind at the Tremont House, in Washington.

After the severe three years' prostration ended, Miss Carroll inquired for this trunk and box, and learned that the Tremont House had gone into other hands after the death of Mr. Hill ; that all its contents had been sold off, and to this day she has sought in vain to learn what has become of that box and trunk. They contained a great number of letters, a completed history of Maryland, and her materials for several projected works.

Thus, through the cruel neglect she had experienced, the world has lost the benefit of works which, from her exceptional ability and her exceptional opportunities, would have been of inestimable value to our future literature.

If any one knows of the fate of that trunk and box they are requested to send word to Miss Carroll or to the present writer, and if ever that history of Maryland comes to light it will be claimed for Miss Carroll, as there are internal evidences which would establish its identity.

Governor Hicks a few days before his death committed to Miss Carroll all his papers with a request that she would write the history of Maryland in connection with the civil war, and the part performed by him in the maintenance of the Union.

Cassius M. Clay also sent to her his letters and papers desiring that she should write his biography.

During Miss Carroll's long and apparently hopeless illness Mr. Clay's letters were sent for and returned to him.

Another ray of light, too, had come to cheer the invalid. A new power was rising upon the horizon in the growing thoughtfulness and development of women, now banding together in clubs, societies, and confederations, with their own journals, newspapers, and publications, and with the avowed determination of never resting until women, as an integral half of the people, had obtained all the rights and privileges proclaimed in the Declaration of Independence, the granting of which alone could make of our country a sound and true Republic and secure the ultimate triumph of the moral and humane considerations and measures upon which its welfare must depend.

Naturally, when this growing party came to know of Miss Carroll's remarkable work they were not disposed to let it fall into oblivion. It seemed as if the Lord himself had declared for their cause in giving to a woman, at the crisis of the national peril, the remarkable illumination that, so far as human knowledge can judge, had turned the

scale of war in favor of our National Union, and had thus
pledged the country for all future time to the just recognition of the equal rights of women as an integral half of
the people, and of equal importance with their brethren to
the welfare of the State. Every effort may be made to
ignore and hide the remarkable fact, but the work of the
Lord remains steadfast, immovable, and incapable of lasting defeat.

> "The moving finger writes,
> And, having writ,
> Moves on."

A notice of Miss Carroll and her brilliant achievements
had been written by Mrs. Matilda Joselyn Gage and in-
corporated in the history of Woman Suffrage, a considerable work, giving a sketch of the career of many eminent
women. Mrs. Gage also wrote and circulated a pamphlet
calling attention to the case, and Miss Phœbe Couzzins made
great exertions in her behalf. One and another began to
inquire what had become of the woman who had done such
wondrous work for the national cause and had been treated
with such deep ingratitude. Mrs. Cornelia C. Hussey,
daughter of a high-principled New York family of friends,
sought her out, visited her at Baltimore, cheered her with
her sympathy, and, interesting others in her behalf, she
was enabled to strengthen the hands of the devoted sister.
She induced the *North American Review*, of April, 1886,
to publish an account furnished by Miss Carroll, and she
procured the publication of a series of letters in the
Woman's Journal, of Boston, that increased the knowledge

and interest beginning to be felt for Miss Carroll's work.

Petitions began to pour in asking Congress to take action in the case. In 1885 it was taken up by the Court of Claims, and in case 93 may be seen the result. The evidence presented, though remarkable, was by no means as complete as it should have been, owing to Miss Carroll's illness and to the difficulty of now procuring copies of her pamphlets. Consequently, though the judgment rendered makes notable admissions and the *moral assent* runs all through, the court was enabled, through some legal defects, to retransmit the case to Congress for its consideration ; and having once made its decision, the case cannot again come before that court without a direct order from Congress to take it up and try it again.

Looking over the brief at the Court of Claims, made by the late Colonel Warden, I noted this significant passage :

* " It may not be amiss here to submit that the two and only drawbacks or obstacles that we have met to the immediate, prompt, and unanimous passage of an act of Congress in recognition of and adequate compensation for the patriotic services and successful military strategy of Miss Carroll in the late civil war are found first in an obstruction which President Lincoln encountered and which he referred to when he explained to Senator Wade that the Tennessee plan was devised by Miss Carroll, and military men were exceedingly jealous of all outside interference." (House Miss. Doc. 58). " The second obstacle which has

---

* Brief of claimant in Congressional case 93.

stayed us is founded in a (to some men) seemingly insuperable objection, often demonstrated in words and acts
by our legislators—a misfortune or disability (if it be one)
over which Miss Carroll had no control whatever, namely,
in the fact that she is a woman."

It would appear that the decision of the Court of Claims
retransmitting the claim to Congress was considered by
Miss Carroll's friends to be in her favor.

Erastus Brooks writes her at this time:

DEAR MISS CARROLL:

Your "Reminiscences of Lincoln" (a work suggested
by Mrs. Hussey) should, as far as possible, bring out the
words and own thoughts of the man. The subject, the
man, and the occasion are the points to be treated, and in
this order, perhaps.

Again, my old and dear friend, I am very glad and hope
the award will meet all your expectations—mental, pecuniary, and of every kind. The hope of the award to yourself and friends must be as satisfactory as the judgment of the
court.

Yours,   ERASTUS BROOKS.

Miss Carroll showed this letter to Mrs. Hussey, who
copied and immediately published it.

Miss Carroll, who had always been on friendly terms
with General Grant, spoke to him of her claim. They
conversed together concerning her work. He assured her
that he had not been aware of its extent, and advised her
by all means to continue to push her claim. I have seen
the draft of a letter, written by Miss Carroll at this time, to
General Grant in which she alludes to the advice he had

given her to push her claim before Congress. The letter is written in the friendliest spirit and in a tone of touching modesty. It should be here noted that there never was any antagonism between these two who had done such great work for the salvation of their country.

Cassius M. Clay wrote to the editor of the New York *Sun* the following letter, as published in that journal :

WHITE HALL, KENTUCKY, *March 3, 1886.*

In 1861, as soon as I could get General Scott apart from his staff of rebel sympathizers, I advised him to reach the Southern forces by all the water-ways, as the shortest and most practical lines of attack. This advice was hardly necessary as every tyro in the Union Army would probably have done the same. But it belonged to Miss Anna Ella Carroll to project and force upon the bewildered army officers—Halleck, Grant, and others—the cutting in two of the Confederacy by way of the Tennessee river by means of the gunboats, and of our facilities of thus concentrating troops and supplies. It was the great strategical coup of the war.

I call the attention of the American nation to Miss Carroll's article in the April number of the *North American Review* of 1886. It appears that the splendid conception of this project called for the immediate reward of a grateful Congress as the representative of the whole people. But when it was found that it was neither Grant, nor Halleck, nor Buell, but a woman, who showed more genius and patriotism than all the army of military men, the resolution was suppressed and the combined effort of many of the ablest men of the Republican party could never resurrect it. Miss Carroll merely states her case. There is no event in history better backed up with impregnable evidence.

CASSIUS M. CLAY.

Mr. Clay also wrote to Mrs. Hussey the following letter, which she sends me for publication:

April 12, 1886.

C. C. HUSSEY.

DEAR MADAME: Your letter and circular of the 8th inst. are received. I was a long time a correspondent of Miss C., never having seen her, but holding a letter of introduction from Vice-President Henry Wilson. I have no standpoint in politics of influence now. * * * Miss Carroll's case shows the infinite baseness of human nature—how few worship truth and justice. I am already assailed for speaking a word in her cause, and shall have all the old feuds against me revived; but I am not dependent upon the American people for subsistence and am not a petitioner for money or office, so I speak my mind.

Very truly yours,

C. M. CLAY.

Miss Katharine Mason, Miss Anna C. Waite, Miss Phœbe Couzzens, Mrs. H. J. Boutelle, Mrs. Louisa D. Southworth, Mrs. Esther Herrman, and a host of other prominent ladies in succession took up the cause, publishing articles east and west, and speaking upon the subject or contributing in some way to the cause. Petitions to Congress continued asking attention to Miss Carroll's case, and that due recognition and award should be accorded to her. High-principled Senators and Representatives would take up these petitions and present them with their own endorsement of the case. But ten righteous men count for little among a mass of Senators and Representatives wildly pushing their own individual and party measures. Every human being with a ballot might be worthy of their attention, but a disfranchised class must go to the wall. With every extension of the ballot such a class sinks deeper and deeper in the scale, and the disregard and contempt for women and their claims becomes inborn—for law is an educator.

In the spring of 1890 Mr. and Mrs. Root spent weeks in Washington verifying, step by step, the incontrovertible facts of Miss Carroll's work. The *Woman's Tribune*, of Washington, generously published a large edition of their report, enclosed advanced sheets, with a personal letter, to every Senator and Representative, and laid them upon their desks, with the invariable result of continued neglect.

Mrs. Abby Gannett Wells, of a highly cultivated Boston family, took up the cause with enthusiasm, made a tour among the army relief posts, and created among soldiers and soldiers' wives a lively interest in the work of their great coadjutor. Tokens of recognition were sent to Miss Carroll, and many a retired veteran, beside his evening fire, put down his name to petitions for her just recognition. Then this brave lady made another effort. She published in the Boston *Sunday Herald*, of February, 1890, an account, from which we give the following extract, having already given extracts from the earlier portion :

"In the last year so many women throughout the country had come to take an interest in this case, petitions to Congress asking for Miss Carroll's suitable recognition and remuneration were sent in considerable numbers, some being presented in the Senate by Mr. Hoar and some in the House by Mr. Lodge. In September last, at an interview with these gentlemen in Boston, I learned it to be their opinion that if I made a plea in Miss Carroll's behalf before the two Congressional Committees on Military Affairs an interest might be aroused to lead to successful results. I therefore promised to visit Washington, and went to the city in the second week in February of the present year.

"The bill calling for an appropriation from Congress for Miss Carroll's services during the civil war, such services consisting of the preparation of papers used as war measures and the furnishing of the military plan for our western armies, known as the plan of the Tennessee campaign, had already been presented in the Senate by General Manderson, of Nebraska, and in the House by Mr. Lodge, of Massachusetts. As Mr. Hoar was ill when I arrived in Washington, he wrote a letter to Mr. Manderson, asking for an early hearing for me, and then sent his private secretary to conduct me to that gentleman in person. I write particulars of the obtaining of these hearings simply to show that even a case demanding urgent action like this finds unexpected obstacles that threaten to retard it indefinitely.

" Mr. Manderson met me kindly, but stated that the committee had such a pressure of business on hand it seemed impossible to take time for Miss Carroll's case, greatly as some of the members had it at heart. But on my replying that I represented the wishes of many women, and we could appeal nowhere else in order for this injustice to be righted, he said if I would come to the committee-room on the morning of the 5th I should be given what time was possible. On that morning General Hawley, the chairman, received me pleasantly, but stated, as he introduced me to the members, that it was unusual to give such a hearing, and he trusted that I would occupy only a little time ; but I am glad to add that the committee's courtesy quite exceeded what might be expected of these busy workers. I had over half an hour of their most earnest attention, and if the expressions upon their faces were a criterion to judge by, Miss Carroll's story was not without its effect upon their sympathy and sense of right. I was particularly glad to see such evidences, because among their members were ex-Confederates, Gen. Wade Hampton being one.

"When Mr. Lodge presented me to General Cutcheon, chairman of the House committee, I heard again the plea of overmuch business ; yet the concession was made—I might come on the morning of the 7th and occupy a "few minutes." Promptly at the hour I was at the committee-room, and since the time was to be so short I had put aside my notes and was telling of Miss Carroll's work, and growing sure of the interest of my listeners, when the chairman interrupted, saying that it now occurred to him that a bill asking for an appropriation belonged with the Committee on War Claims. A book was consulted, and it became the opinion of the committee that this bill did belong with the War Claims Committee. As, in order for me to appear before that committee, the bill would have to go back to the House and be remanded there, and there might be some delay about it, the Military Committee passed a unanimous vote asking the Committee on War Claims to hear my plea at their next meeting, in view of the bill not appearing until later.

"This was discouraging, and the matter grew more so when, on meeting General Thomas, of the War Claims Committee, I was assured that the bill could not possibly belong there. By good fortune I met General Cutcheon at one of the doors of the ladies' gallery of the House, and I told him the dilemma. He generously went to the Speaker and got his decision, which was that either committee could decide as to the merits of the bill. Being given my choice, I decided to appear again before the Military Committee.

"That brought the hearing round to the 11th, the limit of my possible stay in the city. When a quorum had assembled General Cutcheon stated the case, and I was about to begin, when a member objected. He was sure that the bill belonged with the Committee on War Claims. A second member expressed himself as decidedly. A short discussion took place, the vote was put, it was against me and I was dismissed.

I turned away, having never had in my life a greater sense of disappointment. Had I not known that the objection was so purely technical I could have borne the situation better; but to lose the opportunity for this, return home with my mission unaccomplished, see Miss Carroll herself, and tell her that the effort had been nipped in the bud, it seemed impossible to submit to it.

"Mr. Wise of Virginia, the gentleman who had first objected, now appeared to have a second thought.

" ' Since the lady has come so far, and in behalf of another person, it seems to me we hardly ought to dismiss her so summarily.'

" I hastened to say that the bill had had a similar fate before, had passed and repassed from Military and War Claims Committees until action was wholly prevented.

" Mr. Wise thereupon asked for a reconsideration of the motion. The final result was that a unanimous vote allowed me to present my appeal.

"After this generous action I found the presentation of the case a pleasure rather than a duty. It was rather a conversation with liberal-minded gentlemen. When they learned that President Lincoln, his Secretaries, and Senators and Representatives whose names are famous vouched for Miss Carroll's work, the integrity of her claim more surely revealed itself to them.

" The case was ordered to Mr. Wise for special consideration, which he cordially promised to give.

"As I left the committee-room I could not help congratulating myself over the ill-omened beginning, since it had resulted toward a relation of the work far more complete than had otherwise been the case.

" That day I saw the aged invalid for the first time. She is a most remarkable woman still. I heard from her own lips the story I knew so well, but rendered more thrilling than ever as thus repeated ; and I had the happiness of telling her that I believed her case was now in safe hands.

" Not long after, through the unseating of Mr. Wise, of Virginia, Hon. Francis W. Rockwell, of this State, re-

ceived the case as sub-committee. In view of this we
ought to be even more hopeful, since his colleagues, Messrs.
Hoar and Lodge, have put forth so many efforts in its fur-
therance.—*Boston Sunday Herald, February, 1890.*

ABBY M. GANNETT.

The *Century* magazine, which had been publishing an
exhaustive account of " the men who fought and planned
our battles," was appealed to in the name of historical
verity to give an account of Miss Carroll's work. Having
had the matter under consideration for more than a year
and having convinced themselves of the truth of the claim,
they published, in August of 1890, an open letter bringing
the case to the attention of their readers. A public-spirited
lady of Washington purchased copies and laid the marked
article on the desks of Senators and Representatives, with
the same invariable result. But though Congress disregarded
the matter, not so the reading public, and inquiries began
to be made for further information, which it was difficult to
furnish for want of an easily attainable printed account.
It was therefore determined to meet this demand, and the
present relation is the result.

In consequence of the petitions continually received,
friendly Senators and Representatives have again and again
brought in bills asking for $10,000, or even $5,000, for
Miss Carroll's relief (invariably neglected).

Such bills, though very kindly meant, seem to me a mistake. It is not a question of $5,000 or $500,000. It is—
it always has been—a question of *recognition.*

Granted that this wonderful woman by the intense labor of heart and brain, by her whole-souled devotion of life and fortune, has saved the national cause—for the thousands upon thousands of precious lives laid down would have been of no avail had the plan adopted at the crisis of fate been an unwise one—this granted, a noble bill might be acted upon by Congress, but an *ignoble* one—never. Whatever may be our faults, we are at heart a proud and self-respecting people, and no paltry bill would be endured, and no bill which did not award military honor for pre-eminent military services could meet the case with justice and with dignity.

Although weighed down with an immense mass of obsolete law and custom, shall we say that England leads the van in integrity of principle and devotion to human rights? Although the doctrine of divine right was exploded long ago, England loyally holds to her Queen.

As long as it pleases the English people to maintain a royal line, it makes no difference to them whether its representative be a man or a woman. England never had a salic law. But America—when a grand woman comes to her for her deliverance at the crisis of her fate, crowned with heaven's own prerogative of genius, what America does for her in return for her accepted services is to stamp her under foot and bury her out of sight, that her well-earned glory may fall by default upon the ruling class.

Can America continue to be so unjust to women? Can it continue to hold them down as a disfranchised class?

Owing to continued petitions, Military Committees were

appointed during this last Congress to investigate Miss Carroll's claim.

I have not heard the result, but again Congress has adjourned without taking action. About March 27 I had the opportunity of looking over the file which had just come back from the Senate Committee. First of all came a surprising number of petitions sent in during this past year; then the documents in evidence of the claim. They were a meager lot compared to what they should have been. In a case of this importance one would suppose that a copy of every memorial and of every report should have been on the file. Not at all. Quite early in the history of the case "supply exhausted" was the answer given to every request for these documents, and Miss Carroll herself was unable to obtain them.

The reprint of a few of the earlier ones by no means represents them, and owing to the universal exclusion from the Congressional indexes of the later and more important ones, especially the memorial of 1878 and Bragg's report thereon, much important evidence was wanting. Still considering that all that has been printed by "order of Congress" is guaranteed, I should have thought that the evidence given before the Military Committee of 1871 would have been sufficient. Certain I am that if a woman had been on that committee the matter would have assumed more prominence, and there would have been a research for the additional documents that have been omitted. It is the old, old story that every intelligent woman is coming to understand, that you cannot leave to others the interests of a disfranchised class.

In looking over the file at the War Department I noted that there had been inquiries from committees asking if there was a letter of Miss Carroll's there of November 30, 1861, and others mentioned, and the answer returned was " *no.*" It would be in place here to call attention to the fact that they had once been on file there, and the reason that they are there no longer is given in the memorial of 1878, on the evidence of Wade, Hunt, and others.

On April 16, 1891, at the file-room of the House, I saw the file that had come back from the House Committee of this past Congress, whose attention also had been called to the subject in consequence of the many petitions received by the House as well as by the Senate. I counted twenty-five petitions with numerous signatures, as well as some detached letters. An interesting petition was from one of the Army Posts, signed by soldiers and by officers, asking for award to their great co-adjutor. I noted a statement in one of them that the widow of one of the Generals employed in carrying out the Tennessee campaign had been in receipt, ever since her husband's death, of a pension of $5,000 a year, while the great projector of the campaign had been left neglected. Asking if there was anything more, another bundle of petitions was handed to me, each package containing a paper, with extracts from the memorials and reports, neatly arranged, giving some of the remarkable letters of Scott, Wade, and Evans, and the decisions of the Military Committees fully endorsing the claim. It would seem that the committees were appointed to receive the petitions, not to consider evidence, as the documentary evidence was not here on the file. And why should they consider it, when the case had been at the first examined carefully, tried, and a unanimous vote had endorsed the claim, and succeeding reports, including the one mistakenly marked as "adverse," all bore witness to the incontestable nature of the evidence. To go on trying a case so established over and over for twenty years would be a manifest absurdity.

And thus the case stands.

In reading these records a sorrowful thought must come into every woman's soul as she recognizes how deep must have been the feeling against women to prevent Congress, in all these years, from coming to a fair and square acknowledgment of the truth.

But a different spirit is coming over the world: A spirit of justice, a spirit of brotherly kindness towards women, shown in innumerable ways and recognized by them with gratitude and joy.

The active men of to-day were children when the Union was saved. Helpless children, when Miss Carroll, in the prime of her life and fullness of her powers, with clearness of perception, with firmness of character, with the light of genius upon her brow, devoted her time, her strength, her fortune, and her great social influence to the national cause that the men of to-day might have a country, proud, prosperous, and peaceful, to rejoice in themselves and to hand down in unbroken unity to their children.

It should be not only a duty but a blessed privilege—still possible—to see that all that earth can give to brighten the latter days of our great benefactress shall be given her.

That she shall be crowned with the undying love and gratitude of a great and a united nation.

And let us remember, too, what it would have been for our country if the noble daughter of Governor Carroll had thought it her duty to keep out of politics while her country was perishing, and to regard the military movements, upon which its life depended, as something outside of a woman's province.

The nation belongs to its women as surely as it belongs to its men. All that concerns its welfare concerns them also, and nature has gifted them with especial attributes of heart and intellect to aid in its guidance and to aid in its salvation.